Confessions OF A Lonely Soul

ALSO BY HAROLD L. TURLEY II
Love's Game

Confessions
OF A
Lonely
Soul

HAROLD L. TURLEY II

SBI

STREBOR BOOKS

NEW YORK LONDON TORONTO SYDNEY

SBI

Strebor Books
P.O. Box 6505
Largo, MD 20792
http://www.streborbooks.com

ISBN-13 978-1-59309-054-8
ISBN-10   1-59309-054-4
LCCN 2005920451

First Strebor Books trade paperback edition June 2007

Cover design: www.mariondesigns.com

10 9 8 7 6 5 4 3 2 1

Manufactured in the United States of America

For information regarding special discounts for bulk purchases, please contact Simon & Schuster Special Sales at 1-800-456-6798 or business@simonandschuster.com

Our life is a gift from God,
what we do with that life
is our gift to God.

Dedication

I dedicate this novel to the memory of the woman who showed me what true love really was, Lillian Mary Dent Milner. Grandma, you were my best friend and not a day goes by that I don't miss your presence. You stressed to all of us the importance of family and for that your family truly loved you. The past year and a half has been one of the hardest of my life but your presence in my heart makes it a little easier. I know you are enjoying your time with granddaddy again and though I'd love to be selfish and have you still here with me, I know I'll see you again. That's why I can sing, *"This little light of mine, I'm gonna let it shine. This little light of mine, I'm gonna let it shine. This little light of mine, I'm gonna let it shine. Let it shine, let it shine, let it shine."* I love you, Grandma!

Sincerely,
Your Grandson

Acknowledgments

First and foremost, I'd like to thank my Christ and Savior. Through you ALL things are possible.

I knew I'd forget someone in my acknowledgments last go-round and sure enough I did. They made sure to point that out too. I promised not to miss you this time around so to make sure I don't I'm going to get both of you out of the way first.

I'd like to thank my second mother, who is like no other, Ms. Elisa Scott. Ms. Lisa I can't count all that you've done for me so I won't even try. Years ago, you took a 22-year-old kid into your house and treated him no better or worse than your own flesh and blood. Even when things did not work out between your daughter and me, you still remained in my corner and continued to be one of my biggest fans. I want you to know that I appreciate you and all that you do. Most people aren't blessed with one loving parent, I'm thankful enough to say I have two loving mothers. I love you, Ms. Lisa.

To Keesha Trammell, hey miss lady. Though you didn't help out on this project at all, I wanted to at least thank you for being my friend. You made it a point to stress the fact that I forgot to mention you helped edit *Love's Game*. Well, you can't say I left you out anymore.

To my mother Anna and her husband, Mike, y'all always find a way to put a smile on my face. Mike, for so long my mother has yearned for the loving of a good man. Finally I can say she has that. Don't stop being the man that you are and continue to put that smile on her face; get your mind out the gutter. I wasn't talking about in that fashion, Mike. Shit!

Ma, if I put all my thanks, appreciation, and gratitude down on paper for all that you do and have done for me, that would be another ten books in itself. You know what you are to me and how much you mean to me. We both know I'd be nothing without you. Thank you for having a boy and raising a man; not every woman can do that!

To my children, Tre, RaShawn, Malik, and Yhanae, though each one of you finds a way to pluck every nerve I have, you also find a way to touch my heart in every imaginable way too. The day each of you were born, brought me the true definition of unconditional love.

I have to thank Teresa for being a part of my life. No, let me thank Christ for blessing me by placing you in my life and thank you for sticking around even when I get in my moods. You have shown me things I never thought were possible and have me looking over the hills and beyond the horizon. As Babyface would say, "You are soooooooooo beautiful, TO ME! Can't you see... You are everything that I hoped for and you are everything I need... You are so wonderful, TO ME!"

To Zane, wow, what do I say to you? You are more than a publisher to me. You are my friend. Throughout this whole process with *Confessions of a Lonely Soul*, you have been more than supportive, though I was late, and made sure I did what was best for me while dealing with all that was going on in my life. I can't say most people would have done that, yet alone publishers. I'm proud to say I'm one of your authors and a part of the Strebor Family. Simon & Schuster, man, y'all really found a gem in her but I'm sure you already know this by now.

My Strebor Divas...Darrien Lee, Tina Brooks McKinney, Shelley Halima and Allison Hobbs, wow, each of you have touched my life in your own way. I look up to each of you and treasure the knowledge you bestow upon me. I love each of you and if you ever need anything, I'm only a phone call away.

My Strebor Family, we've grown so much over the last couple of months I'm not even going to attempt to list each and every one of you but know that we are about to take this literary world by storm.

I have to thank my advance reader, Luciana Wilson (China), for reading over my manuscript and offering advice and much needed criticism. China, I know you better get to working on your own project. That also goes for my good friend, Natasha Brown. Thanks for being my friend, boo, but just as you've supported my career I'm trying to support yours. Finish that manuscript because you have a voice that needs to be heard.

I'd like to thank my sisters not by blood but rather life, Vonita Alston, Taledia Overton, and Joanna Lawrence. I count on all three of you in more ways than you know. Vonita, I haven't forgotten about the cash I owe you either. Look at it this way though, as long as I owe you, you can never be broke. Taledia, though we don't talk as much as we used to, the love is still there. You know whenever you need anything; you can always call on me. Joanna, we started out as just co-workers and turned into so much more. You understand me like most don't and know how to get me to see things from a woman's point of view. I've always said someone was distracting God when he created you, because you are a man trapped in a woman's body. No wonder you know so damn much! Oh yeah, give my man Kenneth another chance. He is ready now. If not, let him read this. Kenneth, you better stop faking and get my Joanna a three-carat princess-cut from Helzberg. She deserves it and YOU and I both know it.

To Francine and Tiffany, I didn't forget either of you this time. Y'all both know that I look at you like family too. You need it and I got it, so do you. Don't ever forget that.

To my Ms. Ebony Saunders (it's Sanders Harell J, I know!), you know I love you. Though we have been beefin' for the past two years, I really miss you. I've always looked at you as a very good friend of mine and a part of my life. I'm glad to see you and JP "Lil" Jerry found each other again. Now maybe both of you can sit down with Jalen and explain to him why his head is swollen. Damn, that boy got a big head!

To all my little babies out there, I love you and keep on giving y'all momma's hell. People wonder why I love other people's kids so much, it's because eventually they go home. My angels: Dayja (your God-Daddy loves you, baby); Jada (I haven't been able to be around you as much as I'd want to because your daddy wanted to move his ass all the way out to

Montgomery County and now he's bunned up in VA but you know you can always come over and terrorize my house like you always do); Ciara and Alexis (man, each day is an adventure with both of you but I wouldn't have it any other way); Ciara, I can't call you a little princess anymore because you are turning into such the young lady. Alexis, we still have some work to do… I'm just playing (girl, you know you are special); JaNayshia (keep giving your momma and daddy hell and you'll stay Uncle Harrid's favorite); JaVaughn (boy, if you keep waking me up at 6 a.m. on a weekend it's going to be me and you); and Diamond (baby, I fell in love with you the moment I saw you even though you threw up all over my bed. I'll watch you anytime to give your momma and Steve some "Alone Time." Just don't be antisocial like your momma.).

To my little soldiers: My nephew, Tyree (boy, you are just bad for no reason at all and I love it because you are giving Shante all the shit she gave me and then some); Jalen (I'm glad to see you finally grew into your head, boy. It didn't make no sense how big your head was, boy. We used to have to cut your shirts open just to get them on you); and JaVaughn (I don't feel like hearing your aunt's mouth so I won't say nothing negative. I just know it wasn't normal for a nine-month-old to be wearing a 4T and have a full grown beard. Damn, you are a big ass boy). As y'all can see, Harold loves the kids.

Hey Tay, I didn't forget you. Lil Sis, I'm glad you have found happiness with your man but you are still a sucka punk! You jive-time turkey. Always know you have a friend in me if you ever need it. Don't ever forget that!

To my homie Ms. Laura, we miss the hell out of you. You are the only woman who is younger than me that commands so much respect I call you Ms. Me and Tee are going to have to make our way out to Arizona to visit soon. A brother can get his Tiger Woods on out there on the golf course.

To my homies from around the way, man, keep doing y'all thing. They say there aren't too many good dudes out there who know how to take care of their families but all of y'all are proving them wrong. Romeo, Greg, Ray, June, Reggie, James, Mike, and Smiley, take a bow. Lil Dawg aka Lil Dave Chappell, stop drinking those sperm shakes and maybe you can have a family of your own. Naw, you my little homie and you know it. Keep them laughs coming because are you a funny-ass cat!

To my man Eddie, you are a real cat. There aren't too many dudes out there that take on that role as a father for a child that isn't their own. You are a real dude and gets much respect from me. Keep doing what you are doing, pal, except I'm going to need you to step your Madden game up. I'm getting tired of beating you all the time.

Breadwinna Entertainment, all of you are some talented cats and just like I plan to get this book world on lock, I know y'all are going to do the same with the rap game. Money Green, Ron O' Neal, and Peeps, keep doing your thing. My man C, keep making them hittin' beats that have the ladies rocking in their sheets.

To my readers, I would be nothing without you. As long as you promise to continue to read my books, I promise to keep delivering powerful stories with real life situations that need to be talked about.

I want to thank my online world, Readincolor, RAW4ALL, and Writersrx. Y'all give me a place to vent and express my thoughts and a brother needs that.

I have to thank two people who are a truly blessing. I want to thank Ms. Shanae Jones and Mrs. Monique. I call y'all the Strebor stalkers because it don't matter where we are, y'all are there supporting us all the way. I, for one, am so thankful. Y'all are like the parent who is in the stands of your child's basketball game with that big-ass sign with his name on it cheering the loudest! EMBARRASING!!!! Sorry, I was having another childhood flashback. LOL. Naw, y'all are #1 in my book and I am YOUR biggest fan.

Hey, I did it last time so I know I'll do it again but I know I'm missing someone and I don't want anyone to feel unappreciated. At this time, I would like to thank everyone who has given a helpful hand or stood in my corner throughout this whole process. Your encouraging words, many talks, advice, and constant appreciation was much needed and will be forever treasured.

I have to thank all the haters out there. Your negativity is what pushes me to prove you wrong with each and every book. It was said I couldn't write an interesting book about HIV and make it readable without it being boring. I think I did that and then some. I love y'all because each one of you is the air beneath my wings. Your hate pushes me when I start to doubt myself. So please, keep hating while I keep writing.

And finally, I have to thank the woman who taught me and our entire family the true definition of love and the importance of family, Lillian Milner. Grandma, not a day goes by that I don't think about you. I miss you so much. You were and still are my best friend. You are the only woman, outside of my mother, who truly understood the real me. Each day it gets a little easier only because with each passing day, I'm one day closer to seeing you again. From all of your kids, grandkids, and great-grandkids, WE MISS YOU SO MUCH!

Until the next book, peace and blessings—

Harold L. Turley II

Chapter 1

No one knew what to expect. No one knew what to think. All anyone could think about was the fact that I was alive talking, laughing, and joking last week. Now today, they were here to bury me. Life was unpredictable like that at times.

My mother, accompanied by her husband, my brother, my sister, and my in-laws, walked into the church. They were deep in mourning. My mother dropped to her knees at the sight of my closed casket. Pictures of me filled the church. No parent wants to live the nightmare of outliving one of their children.

On top of that, I was her eldest. Each step closer to the casket brought back a different memory. She remembered the first day she brought me home from the hospital. My first step. My first day of school. My first grade-school crush. The day she caught me having sex. The day I graduated from high school. The day I graduated from Towson University. My wedding day. Finally, probably her most treasured memory, the night I performed in front of twenty-one-thousand screaming fans.

The tears poured down her face. She no longer tried to hold them back. Being the strength of our family, her emotion was just what most of the family needed. They needed that sense of it was OK to cry. It was OK to mourn the loss of a friend, relative, or confidant. Finally, she approached my casket, laid her arms across it, and did the only sane, rational thing that entered her mind. She prayed.

"Dear Heavenly Father, please look after my son as he makes the journey from the flesh into the spirit. Please guide him throughout and never leave his side as You've never left mine. Look after my family, Father, during our time of grief and give us the strength and the will to see us through. In Jesus' name, I pray. Amen," she whispered as she lay still on my casket.

She felt a calm come over her spirit. Though she was deep in mourning, she knew that everything was in Christ's hands and she'd be alright. She wiped the remaining tears from her eyes and took her seat. The rest of my immediate family followed to pay their final respects. Finally, they sat down and watched as the church began to fill with friends and distant relatives.

At one, Reverend Young started the ceremony. Even in death I found a way to be late for something. The funeral should have started at eleven-thirty but it seemed as if the steady stream of people never stopped. The church was packed to capacity. I would have never thought I would have touched so many lives.

Reverend Young approached the podium. "Good afternoon, church! We are here today to celebrate the life of DeMarco Montreal Reid. Not to mourn his death, but to celebrate the *life* of a man who devoted his time and energy to bring laughter in the lives of anyone he came in contact with.

"I can remember the first time I attended one of his many sold-out shows. He had the audience literally in tears from laughter. What I remember most about the event was the way he used comedy to educate us on HIV, AIDS, and other social issues. He used his platform to educate, not merely for his own personal gain. That spoke volumes to me.

"He taught me that neither HIV nor AIDS are a death sentence. Simply twists and turns brought on by *life*. I can still hear him saying it now, 'Life is such a strong, powerful, but yet unappreciated word. Life!' He had the ability to bring many emotions out of anyone. He'd make you laugh. He'd make you cry. He'd make you angry. He'd make you happy. But most importantly, he'd make you think. He reminded us not to live for our future but rather in the present, since the future isn't promised to any of us.

"A lot of you are probably wondering, why? Why did the Lord have to take him away from us at such an early age? If you've come today seeking an answer, it will not come from me. Go to the Lord and He will not only provide you with the answer, but also give you the strength to see you through.

"Now I promised Brother Reid I wouldn't preach to you today. When he came in my office and laid down all these rules of how he wanted his funeral to go, I thought he must have been out of his mind. I just knew he was a couple cards short of a full deck. Then, I had to remember the type of man Brother Reid was. I hate to disobey his wishing but when Christ puts something on your heart you want the world to know.

"Go to Him! When you are up late at night and wondering why Marco is no longer here, call Him! When you are lying on the couch watching TV and you think about one of the many memories Marco left you with and the depression starts to set in, GO TO HIM! When life seems as if it has you down and the struggles of life won't let you back up, GO TO HIM.

"No matter what the cause, no matter what the occasion, no matter what the question or the situation go to Him and *He* will provide you the resolution. He will solve the problem! He will ALWAYS be in your corner. He ALWAYS will be on your side. Church, just please... GO TO HIM!"

Reverend Young stepped back from the podium to the sound of "Amen's" and "Hallelujah's" throughout the church. Everyone was so caught up in her mini-sermon that no one even noticed the large overhead projection screen coming down.

"Let the church say amen!" I yelled to the audience on film. "I better not say that too loud. I don't want ReShonda suing me for using the title of her book. Hold up, I'm dead. What can she do? Let the church say AMEN!"

I cracked up with laughter on screen. Some of the audience joined me. They knew I was referring to the author, ReShonda Tate Billingsley, who wrote a very powerful novel called *Let the Church Say Amen*.

I calmed down and continued, "Everybody, cheer up! I know this is my funeral and all, but damn, my body isn't even cold or in the ground yet.

"Let me first apologize for not allowing anyone to say a few good things about me and speak on how I touched them and yada yada ya. No, I've always been different and I'm not going to stop now, not even in death. I don't want any of you crying. The ushers have instructions to escort anyone out of here who they spot crying.

"I'm just playing, but seriously, I'm in a much better place now. It's a little hotter down here than I thought. Okay, let me stop! Seriously though, it's nice up here. Me and Tupac are going to my Welcome to Heaven after-party over at Nat King Cole's jazz club tonight. The drinks could be a little better. All they serve is water or wine, no Remy.

"The wine is strong, I'll give them that, but you know how a brotha loves him some Remy. I can't complain too much, because Jesus sure does know how to throw a party; and the fish, man, the fish is off the hook. Talk about a fish fry, man, it's another level up here.

"Ma, you were right about Christ. Jesus is a black man. I wouldn't have known for real but then he got on the dance floor and it was official. My man can really cut a rug. I thought I'd lost my mind when he started the Electric Slide line over at Nipsy's club last night."

My cousin, Tia, burst out laughing loud enough for someone across the street to hear her.

"Tia, it's not that damn funny sweetie!" I said.

She stopped, astonished, wondering how I knew she was laughing from beyond the grave.

I continued, "I'm willing to bet my last dollar that Tia was the first one to start laughing hysterically. It doesn't matter where we are or how corny the joke is, Tia will find a way to laugh as if Eddie Murphy was on stage doing his rendition of *Saturday Night Live* or *Delirious*."

People in the audience started nodding their heads in agreement.

"We could be at a funeral and everyone is in there crying but she will find a way to laugh about something somebody said. Hold up! We're at a funeral right now. Humph!"

The crowd all laughed.

"But seriously folks, Tia, your laughter is needed throughout the world. You have the gift to be able to see the bright spot in the darkest of clouds. You never let anything get you down and always find a way to find the positive out of every situation. I love you for that."

"I love you too, boo," Tia replied as tears began to stream down her face.

"I hope all of us can follow Tia's example on how to deal with a crisis or a tragedy when you deal with my passing. Some of you will miss me, mostly because I owe a lot of y'all money but make this a happy occasion. I was able to do what the Lord placed me on this earth to do. Don't think about the fact that I won't be acting a fool at any more family reunions. Instead, remember the times I was able to share with all of you. If all else fails, be happy that I'm up here with Tupac and Marvin Gaye cutting a rug at Club Nazareth every Tuesday and Friday night."

People were really laughing now. My funeral seemed more like a show at a local comedy club instead of a funeral at church. People were laughing so hard they were gasping for air.

"Okay, I better stop before my mother tries to kill herself so she can come up here with her switch. Mama, don't do it! You can't come back if you do. There you go. See that smile on your face right now? That is how I want you to remember me, with that same smile. I want you to remember me as a man who would do anything to put a smile on someone's face, no matter what the situation.

"I know Reverend Young found a way to preach, even though I specifically told her not to. She probably broke out with the 'Look to the Lord' sermon she always uses; if she did, I also want you to look toward one another as well. Be there for each other and don't judge one another's faults. We are all family and without family we have nothing.

"When I lost Kalia, I no longer had the desire to live. My family tried to give me the strength to keep going but my eyes were closed and I didn't have the desire to open them. It wasn't until Lia spoke to me that I snapped out of it. After that, I saw the light. I had what I needed in order to move on and get past her death. Each one of you helped me to realize that it was alright to mourn her death, but also continue to live my life as she'd want me to. Because of you, I couldn't and wouldn't allow HIV, AIDS, or depression to destroy another family as it did mine."

Everyone looked around in confusion, wondering what I was talking about. As far as everyone knew, no one in our family had either disease. They believed that I had a very close friend who had AIDS which caused me to increase HIV and AIDS awareness through my comedy. That's what I had told them.

"Today, it's time for the truth. I've never told a soul what I'm about to share with each and every one of you. I vowed to take this to my death bed out of respect for my wife but now is the time. One of the reasons why Kalia committed suicide was because she found out she was HIV positive."

Everyone just sat there silently; they were stunned at the bomb shell I had just sprung. It couldn't have been true; not Lia. She would have come to someone. She would have told somebody but she didn't. I knew that was on the minds of many throughout the sanctuary who knew Lia well.

"She decided that instead of facing the challenge of fighting this disease, she'd take the easy route. I sat up countless nights wondering why she never just came to me. Why didn't she let me help her through it? I needed her just as much as she needed me. I also think she didn't want to see me suffer because she gave me the virus."

Mr. Robinson yelled, "That is bullshit! Turn this shit off! I'll be damned if I'm going to sit here and listen to him lying about my daughter like that. She didn't have AIDS. She would have come to me. She would have told us. He is lying because she was miserable with him. That is probably the real reason why she killed herself. It is because of his cheating, not no damn AIDS. She killed herself because of that bastard."

Kenny stood up.

"You call my brother a bastard again and I swear on my life, I'll beat the shit out of your old ass. If my brother says he got AIDS from that bitch, then that's where he got it from."

"Kenny! Sit your ass down. Both of you need to watch your mouth in the Lord's house and show some respect. I'm not going to sit here and listen to either of you being disrespectful at my son's funeral. Right now all of us are shocked and left with a lot of questions that finally someone is trying to provide the answers to. If you can't sit back, listen, and pay respect to my son on his day, then please leave," my mother said, eyeing both Kenny and Mr. Robinson with pain and disgust in her eyes.

Mrs. Robinson added, "Phil, please calm down and just listen to the boy. We have known Marco for over ten years and have never known him to be a liar. Please, just listen to what he has to say."

Everyone settled themselves down while Reverend Young rewound the tape.

"I also think she didn't want to see me suffer because she gave me the virus," the tape replayed. "No matter how much I tried to ease her conscience by telling her that I didn't blame her but rather myself, it didn't matter. She never believed me.

"If I had been more of a husband, instead of trying to further my career, then she would have never gone to another man for attention and comfort. I'll never forgive myself for the pain I caused her or this family. All I could do was live each day in her memory and for our love.

"She was my best friend and my angel. Finally I'm with her again and able to hold her and kiss her. I'm complete and whole again."

I paused as I became choked up, and tears started to come down my face at the memory of the love of my life.

"Mom, Kenny, Mr. and Mrs. Robinson, I'm sorry I've kept this from all of you. I never wanted any of you to look at me differently. I didn't want you to look at me with sympathy rather than admiration. I never viewed this as a punishment but rather a test of my faith and determination. Luckily for me, Ma, you raised me to fight for what I believed. Those beliefs are what enabled me to possibly save lives. How can that not be a blessing?" I paused.

"When Lia left me, I didn't have an answer to a lot of questions. I'm not going to do that to any of you. Today, I'm going to come clean. Today, I'm going to tell all of you the story and let you know what really happened."

Chapter 2

"Catherine, I'm going to need the marketing report on my desk by close of business. There is no way we are going to be ready to launch next week. Have you heard anything from Jim about the mail piece?" I asked my secretary.

"No, nothing official. However the call center has been saying that customers are starting to call inquiring about it," Catherine replied.

"I guess that's a good thing. I'm glad I have something positive to work with because it's my ass that's on the line. Can you get Brian on the phone and get some type of confirmation, please?"

"No problem, don't forget your wife is on line one."

"Shit!"

I picked up the phone. "Hey baby!"

"Hey. Are we still on for lunch today?" Lia asked.

"I'm sorry, baby, but I can't do lunch today. I'm swamped with work."

"Marco, this is exactly the kind of shit I'm talking about. Your ass never has any time for me. This is what, the fifth time you've canceled on me in the last two weeks?" she asked sarcastically.

"Baby, you know if it were up to me, I'd spend every waking moment with you. We have bills to pay and they aren't going to get paid if I'm not doing my job. I know you want to hook up for lunch, but I just can't. How about we go away next month for a week or two? We can call it a second honeymoon if you'd like. We can go down to Miami Beach or fly to the Caymans or something. Whatever you want, angel."

"Please don't insult my intelligence. Next month will turn into next year, and then that will turn into the following year. Don't even worry about it. I'll be fine by my damn self. I just need to stop wanting to do shit with you because the reality of it is, it's not going to happen," Lia replied.

"Baby, I promise. Right now things are just hectic around here. I'm trying to get this promotion we are running off the ground and you know what type of help I get around here. I'm serious this time. I promise next month we are off to wherever your little heart wants to go. How about we go way on the tenth of next month and stay a week?" I asked.

"Are you serious? I'm not trying to get my hopes up only for you to turn around and disappoint me yet again."

"Baby, I'm dead serious. This could be one of my Valentine's Day gifts to you."

"Is that what this is all about? A Valentine's Day gift? Fuck you, Marco, you can kiss my ass! The way you treat me, you need to be flying my ass to Paris for Valentine's Day."

I cut her off. "Okay, I'm not some little nigga from off the street nor one of your little simple-ass girlfriends. Stop cussing at me like that. You know I can't stand it when you talk to me like that. As for your baseless accusation, the tenth is the only day I can get away. Since we'd be gone during Valentine's Day, it only made sense to include the trip as a part of your gifts. I wasn't saying it to say that it would be your *only* gift. I have other things planned for you for Valentine's Day."

She sighed. "I'll accept your tired make-up attempt if you have lunch with me today. I won't bother you for the rest of the week, since you have this big promotion to run."

"Baby, I can't!"

"Fuck it then, Marco! If you don't give a damn about our marriage, then why should I? I'm not going any damn where with you. For what? You don't have time for me, so I don't want to be bothered with your ass."

I started to become upset. "I asked you politely not to talk to me like that!"

"I'll talk to you however I fucking feel like it. I'm sick of having to beg my damn *husband* to spend time with me. He should want to! I mean, I break my damn neck for you and for what? For you to turn me down every time I want to do something with you. I mean, am I asking you for too much? Am I really? Is a little bit of your time too much to ask for? I'm not asking for the whole damn day. I'm asking for lunch. What is that, an hour, maybe two? Who besides you works sixty hours a damn week?"

I ignored her.

"Answer me, who?"

"I'm not saying shit to you because I've asked you repeatedly not to talk to me like you've lost your damn mind and you keep doing it anyway. You can sit here and argue by yourself if you want to. I'm not participating in it."

"And I told *you* I'll talk to you any damn way I please. I'm a grown-ass woman and the last time I checked your name wasn't Phillip Robinson which means you aren't my damn daddy. You know how I know you aren't, because he knows how to treat his wife. He makes sure she knows how much he loves her EVERY DAMN DAY while I have to guess," she replied.

"I'll talk to you later because right now I don't have shit to say to you."

"No, you are going to fucking talk to me now. If I can't physically have lunch with you, I'll use this time to get this shit off my chest!"

I didn't understand her logic.

"This is pointless. You want to stay on the phone and argue? What will that accomplish? What will that prove? It's not going to get us nowhere. It damn sure isn't going to have us sitting at a table enjoying lunch together today."

"Good. Then it will be right where our marriage is, NO WHERE! Because it damn sure isn't going anywhere if we don't spend any time together nor communicate. What are you going to do about that?" she asked.

Catherine walked into my office and interrupted us, "DeMarco, I have Brian on line two. He confirmed everything, still needs to speak with you regarding another issue."

"Thank you, Catherine. Tell him I will be with him in a minute," I replied.

I turned my attention back to my wife.

"Baby look, I don't want to fight or argue with you. Let me take this call and I'll call you back in twenty minutes. That way we both can calm down and finish this conversation without all the anger involved."

"I like my anger. I can see why you wouldn't though since you are the center of it, but I have no problem with it. It's not going to change... You know what, whatever! Take your call but don't even worry about calling me back. I don't want to talk to you anymore either. You can go to hell!"

I sighed, clueless at how to handle this situation.

"Please don't be like that. How about you meet me at Friday's at two-thirty instead and we can sit down and discuss things over lunch? I don't want us to be like this. Not over something as small as lunch."

She laughed. "Yeah, right!"

"I'm trying but what good does it do if you won't meet me halfway? Come on, meet me at Friday's at two-thirty and we'll have lunch. Does that sound good?" I asked again, hoping to make peace.

"Are you serious?"

"Dead ass. Now let me take this call and handle my business before I'm out of a job," I replied.

She relented.

"Okay, I'll be there. Marco, please don't stand me up and come up with a laundry list of excuses, as you always do. I really do love you and want our marriage to work. Right now, I just don't know what to do."

"Baby, I promise I won't. Now, I have to go. I'll see you in a little bit. I love you."

"I love you too," she replied.

Chapter 3

Lia sat at the bar in Friday's wondering what she was still during there an hour after I was supposed to meet her and yet I was still a no-show.

"I must have been out of my mind to believe him. Why the fuck was I thinking shit would actually be different this time?" I am so stupid. I just need to face the music and realize his ass is never going to change. He will never do right by me. All I wanted was one simple lunch. He's probably at work right now, fucking his slut secretary Catherine. *It's a damn shame that she sees MY husband more than I do*, Lia thought.

"Kalia!" someone called out in the restaurant.

I am just so sick of his shit! I'm sick of it!

"Kalia!" Her name rang again louder this time. It broke her train of thought. She turned around and to her surprise it was her ex-boyfriend, Rashaad. She hadn't seen or heard from him in nearly six years.

Damn, he looks good, she thought.

"Hey Lee! How have you been, girl? I haven't seen you in a minute. I'm glad to see you are still sexy as ever though," he said with a devilish grin.

"Thank you. You don't look too shabby yourself." She paused, then continued, "I'm making it so I can't complain. How about yourself?"

"I can't complain either. I'm still over at Santz & Lewis. I made junior partner last year."

Lia smiled. "Wow, that is good. I always knew you had it in you. Success is your middle name."

"I heard you got married a couple of years back, congratulations."

"That is nothing to congratulate me on," she sarcastically mumbled. "Thank you. Yes, my husband and I tied the knot."

Rashaad detected her sarcasm, though she tried to hide it.

"I take it things aren't going so well?" he probed.

She wanted to yell out, *HELL NO!*

Instead she replied, "Oh no, it's not that. Every marriage has its times when things could be better. Mine is no different. Marriage is what it is."

"What do you mean by that?"

"Just what I said. 'Marriage is what it is.' It's not as easy as some might think but nothing worth having ever really is."

He laughed. "In other words, y'all are having problems but trying to work through them?"

Reading between the lines and seeing what was and wasn't bullshit was never a problem with Rashaad. Some might call it a gift. Lia wasn't one of them. She used to think it was a curse back when they were together. That day wasn't any different.

Without putting her business in the streets, she replied, "Something like that."

It was obvious he was starting to get tired of standing. He sat down on the stool next to her. "Do you mind if I join you?"

Since he was already sitting, Lia didn't protest.

He continued with his train of thought. "Problem, huh? That is funny. I'd never think the two of you would have any problems. Especially with the way you turned me down when I begged you not to leave me for him. He must have been the man for you. Now you can see he isn't so perfect."

"You are absolutely right. He isn't perfect, but the last time I checked, your ass wasn't either. If you were, I'd of never met Marco because I would have still been with you," she said in my defense. She continued, "Look I'm really not in the mood to discuss my marriage with you. I might have to deal with his shit but I'll be damned if I'm going to put up with yours too."

"I'm sorry! I wasn't trying to offend you. I guess I'm still a little bitter about how we ended and glad that the two of you are having problems.

Deep down inside, I still care about you. It's not easy thinking that he, and not I, can call you his wife."

The look in his eyes and his facial expression said he was being sincere. She remembered how devastated Rashaad had been when she left and how deflated he looked when she refused to come back.

"Rashaad, you know I never meant to hurt you intentionally. Leaving you was one of the hardest things I ever had to do but it was something that was necessary for me. I didn't want to string you along nor lie to myself about my feelings. My heart belonged to another man and still belongs to him," she said.

"Can I ask why do you feel the need, even now, to emphasize your love for him? I've never questioned it but do you. Do you really love him or is that the real reason why you emphasize it? So you can convenience yourself that you love him and made the right decision by leaving me."

"I'm not even going to answer that. Of course I love my HUSBAND. I'm in love with him and nothing can or will change that. I might wish he'd concentrate more on me than his work but what wife wouldn't want all of their HUSBAND's time. I want to be up under him twenty-four/seven but that isn't possible. I know that and that's what I'm dealing with, not the love for my HUSBAND. Do you hear that? HUSBAND, not boyfriend or man, but my HUSBAND. Please understand, that's not going to change."

Her emotions were starting to get the best of her. She was infuriated but not with Rashaad but rather her husband. She remembered who she was taking her frustrations out on and paused.

"I love him to death. He is my life."

She took a sip of her drink trying to totally recollect her thoughts.

"I'm sorry, I didn't mean to sit here and bore you with my problems. It's just that sometimes I do feel unappreciated. Sometimes, I do feel unloved. Sometimes, I just want to lie around and be held by my husband and it's a little frustrating. Either way, I know you'd much rather talk about something else."

He cut Lia off, "I don't mind at all. When we were together, we could talk about anything. I miss that. I miss just sitting down and talking for hours. How about we get a table, sit down, and have lunch? I don't want to overstep my bounds or anything though."

Every part of her body knew having lunch with him was wrong, but the reality of it was she didn't want to be alone. She craved the attention; it made it easy for her not to find the energy to turn down his request.

"That's fine. It doesn't look like Marco is going to make it anyway, so why not."

***

The time flew past as they ate lunch and enjoyed their casual conversation. It was damn near 6:00 p.m. when Lia reached for her cell phone.

"I know my husband is at home starving and wondering where I am."

The house phone rang and rang but there was no answer.

"Hello, you've reached the Reid residence," she heard the answering machine say. She dialed my work number.

"This is DeMarco," I answered.

"It figures your ass would still be there. What are you still doing at work? Do you know what time it is?"

"Baby, since when have I ever worked a set schedule? I told you I'm trying to get everything straight for the promotion for our phone service product we are about to launch," I replied.

"Marco, you have been at work since what, six-thirty this morning. It is time for you to bring your ass home."

"Lia, I can't have this discussion with you right now!"

She cut me off, "Just like you couldn't have lunch with me today or how about like you couldn't even pick up the phone and call me and tell me you weren't coming. You can't have this conversation now like that?"

Fearful of another argument, I quickly apologized. "Look, I'm sorry about earlier, baby. Things got hectic around here and certain things needed my attention."

"I guess me needing it wasn't important," she quickly replied.

"I'm not saying that, baby. Right now I honestly can't talk to you about this. I have a ton of shit that I have to finish before I leave here tonight."

"You are a got-damn grown-ass man. I don't want to hear that bullshit! You can do whatever you want. If you want to leave, then your ass can put your coat on and fucking leave!"

"Okay, I can see exactly where this conversation is going. I've told you before about talking to me like you've lost your mind. I'll be home when I'm finished here. Bye!" I said and hung up the phone.

She couldn't believe I actually hung up on her.

What the hell is his problem? Who the hell does he think he is? I'm the one begging for attention, can't he see that? she asked herself.

"What's wrong?" Rashaad asked as if he hadn't heard everything.

"Nothing, everything is fine."

"Lee, I'm not stupid. You don't have a heated debate with your husband about being stood up if everything is fine. Talk to me so I can help," he pleaded.

"There is nothing to talk about. My husband is at work and I'll be sleeping alone again tonight."

"That is a start, let's talk about it."

"Talk about what? I'm okay. I'm just going to go to the bathroom and freshen up, then go home. If you're not here when I get back, don't worry about the check. I'll take care of it."

"First of all, I'm not going anywhere. I'll be right here when you get out and second, the check is already taken care of. Now go handle your business and get yourself together so we can finish our evening."

She couldn't help but smile. She hadn't felt this way in a long time. She got up and went into the bathroom.

"Why can't my husband act like this? Why can't he be the one sitting out there right now instead of Rashaad? Since he doesn't want to be the one sitting out there, I'll just enjoy the company of who is. At least he wants to spend time with me and talk," she said to herself in the mirror.

She could remember a time when we would sit around and just talk for hours. There was a time when she felt like she had a husband who treasured the ground she walked on. Now it seemed more like she had a roommate she just lived with. There was no companionship, no marriage really.

The bathroom door opened and Rashaad stood at the entrance with a devilish grin on his face. He locked the door so no one could come inside and interrupt what was running through his mind.

Lia didn't protest. Subconsciously the attention he was giving her turned her on. She wanted him. In fact, she craved the attention. He walked toward her.

"Rashaad, what are you doing?" she asked.

"Shhh!" he said, putting his finger over her mouth. He started kissing on her neck. The warmth of his tongue sent chills down her spine. She knew it was wrong but she wanted to be fucked. He caressed her breast and continued to kiss her neck. Her panties went from damp to soaked.

"Fuck me! Please, just fuck me," she begged softly in his ear.

He picked her up and put her on the sink countertop. She unbuttoned his pants and slid them down with the ball of her foot. Rational thought was now escaping her. She was running on pure emotion and lust. He pulled her panties off and placed himself inside of her. Who would have thought wearing a skirt that day would have been a benefit and a disaster, all in one?

Her body cringed at the enjoyment of his thickness inside her. He took his time with each stroke, wanted to feel her. She didn't want to be made love to though. She wanted to feel him in her stomach. She pulled him in closer.

"FUCK ME!"

He picked up his pace; happy to oblige. After a while, the only sound that filled the bathroom was his pelvis smacking up against her stomach. She was really into it but didn't make one sound. No moaning. No screaming of enjoyment. Nothing but the sound of their bodies meeting one another. This was what she had asked for but not what she really wanted. She wanted to be with her husband and try to save her marriage.

Rashaad pulled out and turned her around to hit it from the back. The feeling didn't change. It felt so good but also so wrong at the same time. No matter how much she pulled her hair or smacked her on her ass, she remained quiet. Her face was motionless. She'd come three times but you would have never known by her actions. Never had she felt like this before. Finally she felt the warmth of his semen on her lower back and it was over. Still there was no feeling or guilt. She felt nothing.

Chapter 4

The entire car ride I'd prepared myself to hear it. I'd messed up but what else was I suppose to do? It's not like the work would finish itself. I decided to take the lesser of both evils. It's not like she would have been any happier if I had been fired and we were out on the street. Then she would have been asking me why the hell I wasn't at work. I had made my choice and the only thing I could do was stick with it.

The sound of Lia crying became louder and clearer with every step I took toward the bedroom door. My heart started to ache. I hated that she was in pain because of me. I had let my wife down again and there wasn't a Hallmark card that would make it right. The shit was thick and I was in it knee deep.

Going into marriage you know you are going to make your share of mistakes along your journey together but I think my actions were taking that overboard. It seemed as if I couldn't do anything right. If I turned left, she wanted me to turn right. If I made her steak and eggs, I should have known she wanted pancakes and sausage instead. Nothing I did ever seemed right anymore. It didn't matter how right I thought I might have been. I was wrong.

I stood outside that door wanting to turn around and run. How could I face her? What would I say? It's not like I was out doing anything wrong, I was at work doing my job. If I told her that, it would only lead to more trouble.

Trying to figure out the right way to handle the situation was more exhausting than just dealing with it. Against my better judgment, I walked into our bedroom.

"Hey," I said. Shit, it was all I could think of at the time. I continued, "Baby, look I'm so sorry about lunch today. I honestly didn't mean to stand you up but I looked up and it was five o'clock. Lunch was way over. I didn't think you would still be at the restaurant."

She started to wipe the tears from her face.

"I'd really like to believe that but not once did you bother to pick up the phone. Maybe time did get the best of you, but why not just pick up the phone and say what you are saying to me now?" she questioned.

"Baby, I can't tell you. I should have but I didn't. Do you know I've been standing outside the bedroom door for the past couple of minutes trying to think of all types of excuses? However, I couldn't think of a single one. I couldn't think of any because there wasn't one that will excuse my behavior."

"Marco, I don't understand you sometimes. I really don't. I mean, do you really want this marriage to work? Honestly, do you? Have you ever just sat back and thought about that?"

"Lia, you are the only woman I want. You're the only woman I've ever wanted. I cannot, I mean, cannot see my life without you in it. You mean everything to me. The reason why I work so hard is to provide a better life for you," I replied.

She smirked.

"Is that so? Marco, do I look like an ass or something to you? I must. I have to because you obviously think I'm one. First, never have I doubted your intentions to provide a better life for us financially, but that isn't the reason why you work all those damn hours. You do it for yourself and the high you get. It stopped being about me and this family a long time ago and you know it."

She was right. There was something about seeing a promotional ad campaign on TV that I created. I got an unusual satisfaction out of being able to say, "I did that."

She took my lack of denial as confirmation that she was correct.

She continued, "Today I sat in that restaurant, ready to call a divorce lawyer. I finally reached my breaking point. I was through until…" She paused to regain her composure. My heart was in my throat at the thought of possibly losing my wife.

She gathered her thoughts and continued, "I was through with you, Marco. I really was. It took fucking another man to truly realize just how much you hurt me. But it also took me to fuck another man to realize how much I'm still in love with you and need you to be a part of my life."

"What the fuck do you mean, you fucked another man," I said, cutting her off.

She smirked. "Hmph, I have you attention now, don't I? I would appreciate it if you wouldn't talk to me like that. You know how much I don't like it."

"You can play around with this situation but I don't find a damn thing funny. What the hell do you mean you fucked another man?" I asked again.

"Either we can talk and I finish what I was saying or we can go our separate ways; the choice is yours."

She paused, waiting for my reply. What choice did I have? I wanted to storm out of that house and say "fuck it" but what would that have solved? Regardless of what she had said, I still would have been in love with her. I motioned for her to continue.

"When we got married, it wasn't for money but for the love and respect we both had for one another. We vowed before God that we would stick with each other in sickness and health, through good times and bad until death do us part. Until DEATH do us part. That doesn't mean you get on my nerves or until you hurt me or until I reach my point of no return but until DEATH do us part."

I cut her off again, "What does any of that have to do with you fucking another man? I mean really. You sitting here talking about 'until death do us part' after you confess fucking another got damn man!"

She shook her head in disgust. "You know this is the most enthusiasm I've seen you show anything dealing with us in what, three years. There is a problem there but I'm sure you won't see it. You're probably more concerned about who I fucked versus anything else I said. It wouldn't surprise me though. You never hear my cries for love, attention, and affection either. Yes, I fucked another man today but who he is, it doesn't even matter."

I was speechless. I didn't know what to say. How was I supposed to take that?

"I don't get you. I mean, what should I be saying? What am I missing? Should I be happy or something that you realized you wanted to be with me after you had sex with another man?"

"Once again you weren't listening. I didn't have sex with him, I fucked him. There is a difference. Now as for how you are supposed to take it, I really don't give a damn, because I didn't have to tell your ass shit. I could have taken that to my death bed," she shot back at me.

That didn't help matters. No matter how she worded what she did to me, it was the same thing. The bottom line was she'd betrayed me. How dare she say we made a vow to one another and, for that, she wants to be with me but breaks that vow by sleeping with another man?

"Why do I get the strange feeling that is supposed to comfort me in some way? No matter how you put it, the bottom line is y'all had some type of sexual contact. I'm not feeling that at all! I would never step out on you! I don't care what the circumstance is: I love your ass too damn much! I would never hurt you like that! Never!"

"You really believe that too, don't you? Sweetie, I hate to be the bearer of bad news, but it seems like you need a reality check. You've been hurting me for a long time now. I'd say the last year and a half at the least. I don't like not being able to talk to you or hold you. I don't like the fact that your co-workers see you more than I do. I'm your wife. I'm the one who should be getting your time, not them!"

Tears started to creep out of her eyes and I finally started to understand the nature of her pain. At that point, everything was starting to make sense.

"Look, we are both about to get emotional. I'm not excusing your actions nor do I want you to excuse me. What I want is my wife so my question to you is how do we move forward? How do we get past this?"

In my mind there were only two options. Either deal with her actions and move on or live my life without her. I wasn't going to live without her, so we needed to find a way to move beyond this.

"I honestly don't know if we can. Don't take this the wrong way because I know you love me but I don't think you know how to love me the way I need to be loved. You love your job too damn much and I'm scared to make you choose. I'm actually afraid of which you'd prefer."

"Then let me ease your mind. There is no choice that needs to be made. You are my world. Nothing comes before you. If you feel like I don't know how to love you, I'm standing right here ready to learn. I'm willing to do anything, as long as I'm with you."

"If you truly mean that, start showing me that nothing comes before me. Spend time with me. I'm scared to even have children with you because of what could possibly happen. Either you'll neglect our child like you do me or you might try to work even harder trying to provide for both of us which still would result in you neglecting our child. I need a husband, not a paycheck. I need a husband."

"I'm not trying to be funny, baby, but I'd think you'd need a husband who brings home a paycheck."

"I know you have to make a living but there is a difference between working and spending your life at work. I just want the same hours you put in at work, also put in our marriage.

"You asked me how we move forward. The real question is, are you going to do what it takes for us to move forward? I want you to think about that before anything else. I mean, really think about it. I don't want you to give me an answer off pure emotion. I want you to sit back and think about what you are going to do in order for us to move forward."

I sat there and thought of the proper response. What could I say to convince her I could once again be the man she fell in love with or, better yet, the one who could love her the way she needed to be loved? What could I do to not only show her that I loved her but also show her how much she meant to me? It finally hit me. No words would ever describe my feelings for her. I'd let my actions do all my talking.

"What am I going to do? I'm going to show you. I'm going to let my actions speak to you in volumes rather than my words. I'm going to spend more time with you so you can see that I want to be with you and do what it takes to make this relationship work. That's what I'm going to do.

"That is the only thing that makes sense to me. I could easily tell you this and that but would you really believe it? I doubt it. You probably don't believe me now, so instead of talking, baby, I'm just going to let my actions speak."

I paused. "I only ask that you be patient and trust me enough to show you first, then make your decision. Don't look at me with closed eyes but with your eyes and heart wide open ready to receive all that I give. If I don't change, then I'll pack my things and leave without a fight."

"Marco, I don't know. I'm scared. You've hurt me so much. How do I not know you won't hurt me again? How do I not know I won't be a fool to trust you again?"

"You don't. That is why I'm asking for time to rebuild your trust in me. Can you do that for me; just give me some time to try?" I pleaded.

"All I've ever wanted is to be your wife and grow old with you. If these actions you speak of will bring me happiness with you, I'll be right here waiting to see them."

I couldn't help but cry. I guess the stress of the whole evening got to me more than I was originally letting on. Lia was my queen and I was treating her like a pauper. She wiped the tears from my eyes and gave me something my body was craving, a hug.

Chapter 5

"Lia," I yelled. "Come on, baby. It's almost eight o'clock. You need to get up or you are going to be late for work. Lia, come on. Get up!"

She barely even budged. Our new morning routine was becoming an old habit for me. It seemed as if with each new day, it became even more difficult to wake her. I hadn't a clue why she was so tired all the time but was starting to get concerned.

I went over to the bed and pushed her until she finally awoke.

"Come on, baby. It's time to get up. You're going to be late. It's damn near eight."

She rolled back over to get comfortable.

"I don't think I'm going to work today. I'm tired and I don't feel good," she replied.

"Baby, you can't keep making this a habit. You stayed home last Thursday for the same reason."

"I know. Come here and give me some sugah before you leave and I'll call you later on when I get up," she replied.

"But baby ??

She cut me off. "Look, Marco, I already told you I'm not going in so can you please come over here and give me my morning sugah. I love you, baby."

How could I resist a request like that? I did what she asked but not without adding my final thoughts.

"Only on one condition, promise me you'll call the doctor and get checked out. I'm worried about you."

"Why? It's probably nothing. I probably need to take some vitamins or something but if it will make you feel better, sweetie, I'll make an appointment for later on today," she replied.

My mind still wasn't totally at ease. I knew something was wrong and I wasn't going to feel better until I either knew what it was or the doctor cleared her and said everything was fine. It just wasn't like her to be so tired and sick all the time.

She had no energy to do anything anymore. At first I thought it was because we'd been spending a lot of time out the past couple of months and her body was starting to catch up with all the activity. But she wasn't just complaining about being tired, but also sick. Something else had to have been causing her to feel this way.

I gave her another kiss and left for work. Though she'd never admit it, I know she was questioning whether something was wrong herself. It was already confirmed she wasn't pregnant because she had taken a pregnancy test a week earlier and it had come back negative. She was crushed when she saw the results. She'd actually had her hopes up and prayed she was pregnant.

She could picture her son playing football in the backyard or following his daddy around trying to mimic his every move wanting to be just like him. She imagined him sitting at the dining room table, frustrated, trying to understand his homework. She saw herself right there helping him. She also imagined a little girl falling asleep on her daddy's chest at night. Going to dance recitals and putting her hair in pigtails. She could envision getting her ready for her first day of kindergarten. The sight of the negative sign on the pregnancy test brought all her hopes and dreams crashing down just as fast as they'd gone up.

She broke out of her daze and called Dr. DeSandes' office to see if she could be fit in. The big fuss I was making about her health was starting to work on her nerves. She was rattled. Since she knew she wasn't pregnant, she had no clue as to what could be wrong. The unknown started to scare her enormously.

***

"Mrs. Reid," the medical assistant said. "You can come back now."

Lia followed her to the examining room.

"The doctor will be with you shortly. Please get undressed and put on the blue gown. You can put your clothes in here," she said, pointing underneath the examining table.

Lia slowly undressed. The room was cold as mystery filled the air. Lia knew something was seriously wrong. Call it woman's intuition.

The doctor walked in the room. "Good morning, Mrs. Reid. What seems to be the problem this morning?"

"I'm not sure, Dr. DeSandes. It just seems like lately I'm always extremely tired and have no energy. I took a pregnancy test last week and it came back negative so that can't be the reason."

"Do you find yourself having to use the bathroom a lot?"

"Yes."

"Are your breasts tender or sore like you are about to start your cycle?"

"Yes."

"Any vomiting or nausea?"

"Yes."

"When was your last cycle and how long did it last?"

Lia thought back.

"I started on February twenty-third and it lasted for five days, I believe."

"That would put you at just a little over a week late."

Dr. DeSandes paused while he thought to himself. He started to write in her medical chart.

"I want to give you another pregnancy test, just as a precaution. I'm not totally convinced you aren't pregnant just yet. It's one thing for you to have a symptom here or there but you seem to be experiencing all of them, plus your cycle is late. Let's just wait and see what the results show first and then we'll go from there."

Lia's heart started to pump with excitement. Her possibly being pregnant was music to her ears. She could give me the one gift I'd prayed for.

As she stood over the toilet putting a sample in the cup like the doctor requested, she tried not to get her hopes up but she couldn't help it. It seemed as if this was the sign she prayed for night after night. Finally it was her time to have a baby. He finally heard her cry and was granting her wish.

She waited nervously in the examination room for Dr. DeSandes to come back with her results. It was killing her inside. As positive as she was trying to think, she couldn't help but worry about being let down again. Doubt now clouded her mind. It seemed as if the longer she waited, the surer she came she wasn't pregnant and her hopes were up for nothing yet again. That bad feeling she'd had earlier had filled her gut yet again.

The door opened and Dr. DeSandes walked in slowly. His posture spoke in volumes. There was no smile on his face. She no longer questioned whether she was pregnant. She now wondered what was wrong with her and how severe it was.

"Okay, Mrs. Reid, we've got back your results and…"

She cut him off. "Is it that bad?"

"It's nothing bad at all, Mrs. Reid. Some might actually call it a blessing. We've gotten your results back and you are indeed pregnant."

She started to cry from excitement and joy.

"Are you sure?"

"I'm positive and I'll prove it. First, I need you to lie back and open your legs," he replied.

Any other person would have found themselves punched in the nose with a request like that but today was different. She happily obliged. Dr. DeSandes pulled the sonogram machine over to her and administered the exam. He pointed to the screen and showed her our baby.

"Here is the baby."

She couldn't believe it. It was true. She was pregnant and was going to have a child. Dr. DeSandes started measuring the baby and taking pictures to get an idea of how far along she was.

"It seems as if you are three to four weeks' pregnant."

None of that mattered to her. She had heard all that she needed to. She was pregnant. He finished the exam.

"Mrs. Reid, we are going to need to draw some blood for routine testing and I want you to schedule another appointment. I want to see you every four weeks for your first trimester, every two weeks for part of your second and third, and every week for your fourth. Would you like to know your approximate due date?"

Lia nodded her head yes.

"It's November twenty-fifth."

She made sure to remember to play the Lotto and play 1-1-2-5 when she left the doctor's office. That was definitely her lucky number. That was the day her miracle was due to be born.

***

She walked into the house high on life. There wasn't anything that could bring her down. She wanted to do something special for me. She could envision how happy I'd be when she delivered the wonderful news. The trick would be making sure it was also memorable.

She whipped up something special for dinner and slipped on her long back dress with the cut-out back. It was my favorite. She set the table with candles for an intimate dinner for two.

Her plans were for us to eat and enjoy each other's company, then tell me the wonderful and life-altering news. She was determined to stick to the script but knew due to her overexcitement it wouldn't be easy.

I walked into the house, tired from a long day. The aroma of steak well done with string beans, corn on the cob, baked potatoes, and corn bread quickly awoke me. If that didn't do the trick, the sight of my beautiful wife standing there in her sexy seductive dress would have.

I walked in the kitchen and my mouth watered while my stomach growled at the sight of my feast. This wasn't Sunday so something had to be up. She was going all out with dinner.

"Baby, what's the occasion?"

"Can't I just want to make my husband dinner and serve it by candlelight?" she asked mischievously.

Now I knew something was up. I must have forgotten one of our many childhood anniversaries again that she cherished. My philosophy was never forget her birthday, the day we met, where we went on our first date, the first time we kissed, the day I proposed, and the day we got married; everything else wasn't important. You couldn't tell her that though. I tried to remember but I couldn't put my finger on what was so special. I tried to improvise.

"Of course you can, but I know you too well, honey, something is going on. What it is, I'm not sure of yet, but it will show its evil head soon enough."

"Evil? I don't know what you are talking about."

She continued the charade as if she had no clue even though it was obvious she did. I couldn't though. I had no idea which of her many special occasions I was forgetting.

"Baby, I'm sorry but I don't know what today is. I try to remember all the little anniversaries that are special to you but I can't."

She started laughing. I didn't find the torture of not knowing what was up funny at all.

"Sweetie, you haven't forgotten anything because I haven't told you yet why today is such a special day."

"What haven't you told me? Why is today so special?" I asked.

Though she planned to sick to the script, I had ruined it. She figured there was no reason to drag it out, now was as perfect a time as any to tell me.

"Sweetie, I'm pregnant!" she said as tears started strolling down her face.

"You're what?" I shook my head in disbelief. "Baby, are you serious? We are going to have a baby?" I asked to make sure.

She nodded her head yes.

"We're going to have a baby!" she replied.

I hugged her and continually kissed her forehead.

"I love you! I love you! I love you! I love you!" I said continually.

It was all I could say. I never loved that woman more than I did that day. She was giving me the gift I wanted most and feared I'd never have. I was finally going to be a father. After that news, her plans for our evening were going to be further altered as I picked her up and took her upstairs.

Chapter 6

The phone rang constantly. I was too tired to even think about moving, let alone answer it. I let her answering machine catch it.

"Good morning, Mrs. Reid, this is Dr. DeSandes. Can you please give us a call to schedule an appointment? I need to…"

I picked up the phone.

"Hello," I said, still sounding half asleep.

"Hi, is Mrs. Reid in?"

"No, she is at work. This is her husband though. Is there something I can help you with. I mean there isn't anything wrong with the baby, is there?"

"No, not at all, Mr. Reid. The baby is fine. I actually was calling to re-schedule your wife's appointment. Unfortunately, I won't be able to see her next week due to a medical conference I'll be attending."

My nerves calmed down.

"Do you have your schedule in front of you now? If so, tell me what you have available and I'll make sure she is there."

He checked for the next available date and I scheduled her appointment. I called her at work and told her she needed to leave work early. I knew how understaffed her hospital was, so I wasn't so sure if she'd actually be able to make it. Thankfully, it wasn't a problem.

You know, for some reason, the minute she found out she was pregnant she had a newfound energy. It had a positive effect on our home life. She was nothing but a bundle of joy now. I couldn't remember being this happy and much in love in a long time. Our relationship finally reached a level both of us relished and truly enjoyed.

Lia arrived at the doctor's fifteen minutes early. They had her go to the bathroom and pee in a cup. Unfortunately, my job wasn't as easy to escape as hers. She surprisingly wasn't mad. With my past of allowing work to consume most of my time she could have easily thought she'd go through this whole process by herself but she trusted me now to do right by her and the baby.

"Mrs. Reid, you can come back now," the nurse said as she opened the door. Lia followed her into the examining room.

The doctor came in as the nurse exited. He completed her monthly exam. He listened to the baby's heartbeat to make sure everything was okay. Once he finished, he asked Lia to come into his office.

"Come on in, Mrs. Reid, and have a seat." He paused. "How are things since last I've seen you?"

"Fine. I can honestly say for once in my life I have nothing to complain about."

"Are you still feeling tired? That is normal for the first trimester."

"I know but actually I've found myself having a lot of energy lately. When I do feel tired or groggy, I force myself to get up and get into something. All I've wanted to do is give my husband a baby and start a family. That is all I need to get me through every day."

Anyone around her could see how much she was glowing and how enthused she was. That is why it troubled and bothered Dr. DeSandes to break the news. Lia picked up on the troubled look on his face.

"Is there something wrong, Dr. DeSandes? Is it the baby?"

He let out a sigh. Lia was now worried. She could sense something was wrong and Dr. DeSandes wasn't giving her any signs that she was over-reacting.

"First, let me say that the baby is fine. We received your blood test results back."

Lia felt relieved with the news the baby was alright but still cautious regarding her test results.

"Okay and what does that mean? Is there something wrong with me? As long as it's not something that will affect my baby, I'm fine. Tell me, doctor," she insisted.

Dr. DeSandes gathered his thoughts. His uneasiness was a dead give-away whatever it was, was something serious. Lia tried to brace herself for the news.

"Mrs. Reid, it pains me to tell you this, but you're HIV-positive."

As the words positive came out of his mouth, she could feel her world shattering before her own eyes. She didn't hear another word he uttered. All she could replay over and over in her mind was *HIV-positive*.

How was she going to tell me? What was going to happen to the baby? How did she get it? Why? Why? Why? She asked herself all these questions.

"Mrs. Reid!" Dr. DeSandes said, breaking her out of her trance. "Are you alright?"

"What do you mean, am I alright? You just tell me that I have HIV and then have the nerve to ask me if I'm okay." She laughed, then continued, "HELL NO, I'm not okay! How the hell am I supposed to tell my husband this? We haven't used protection in I don't know how long, trying to get my ass pregnant and instead I give him HIV and a baby. How do you think he is going to take that? What do I do? Since we are asking dumbass questions, tell me doctor, what I do?" she shouted as tears started to stream down her face.

Reluctant to answer her, Dr. DeSandes got up and went over to comfort her.

"I'm so sorry. I wish I had all the answers to your questions but I don't. If you like, I can tell Mr. Reid for you and suggest he get tested also."

Lia was still too hysterical to reply. On what was supposed to be the happiest day of our lives, somehow misery had found a way to attack the marriage yet again. She wiped her eyes and tried to regain her composure.

"No, I'll tell him. I owe him that much. Is there anything else, Doctor?" she asked.

"Well, I wanted to talk to you more abut the disease and how we are going to treat it. I want to refer you to a colleague of mine who actually specializes in HIV and AIDS treatment in pregnant women."

She cut him off. "Is my baby gong to be okay or will it have HIV too?"

"I honestly don't know and would rather you speak with him about it. He can give you a more accurate percentage of whether or not the baby will contract the disease or not. What I can tell you is that just because you are HIV positive doesn't mean your child will be also."

That was a little comforting, however, it wasn't enough. Dr. DeSandes couldn't speak to a certainty. It was all possibility. Top that off with the news still being fresh, it was all too much for her to handle.

"I'm sorry, Doctor, but I really need to get out of here. I'll call you later and get more information from you. Right now I just need to get the hell out of here and figure out how I'm gong to break the news to my husband."

Dr. DeSandes was very understanding. You'd never have a clue that was his first time delivering news like that to a patient. Lia stormed out of the doctor's office and waited for the elevator in the hallway. She began to cry again.

"How am I going to tell Marco? What have I done?"

✳✳✳

I walked into the door, tired from a long day. I planned to spend my afternoon with my wife at her appointment but unfortunately I spent it at work. After every minute at work, I looked forward to getting home and seeing my wife's beautiful face. She was my sunshine on a rainy day. After today, I needed a dose of my baby and a big one at that.

She was wavering on the bed, asleep. I took off my clothes and curled up next to her. The warmth of her body awoke my manhood. I started to kiss her neck and rub on her breasts. Her nipples started to become erect and protruded through her T-shirt.

I couldn't think of a better way to wake her up other than with my head in between her legs, please her. As I made my way down her stomach to ecstasy, she awoke and started to moan in enjoyment. As I kissed her belly button, I rubbed in between her legs. I could feel her sensuous lips through her stained panties. I started to take them off.

"Stop, baby, stop!" she said and sat up.

I was puzzled.

"What's wrong?"

She didn't say a word. She just sat there staring at the wall. I started back up again. She quickly pushed me out of the way, and then stood up. "Stop!"

I knew something was wrong for sure. I couldn't remember the last time she turned down any form of sex, let alone oral at that. I read about how women become moody and emotional during pregnancy and hoped this was the problem and not the fact that I missed the baby's appointment."

"What's wrong, baby? Did I do something?"

"No, I'm just not in the mood."

She walked into the bathroom and closed the door behind her. I sat up on the bed and tried to figure out what had just happened or what I had done. I wasn't buying the *I'm not in the mood* act she was giving me. I knew her too damn well. Something was wrong and nine times out of ten it was because of something I had done.

All I could think of was me missing her appointment earlier that day because of work. My job was what almost cost us our marriage a few months ago; maybe she thought I was falling back into my old ways. I hoped not, because those days were long gone. My family was my main focus.

Maybe she was testing me earlier by telling me to go to work and skip the appointment. She wanted to see if I'd go along easily or if I'd protest and still come. I started to panic. A million and one reasons cluttered my mind as to what I had done wrong and I hadn't a clue which of them was correct.

The bathroom door opened and out she walked.

"Baby, what did I do? It's obvious something is bothering you. I can't help or correct my actions if you don't talk to me and tell me what it is. Is it because I missed the appointment today?" I asked.

I noticed her face was a little damp as if she had gone into the bathroom to wash away the tears that crept out her eyes. Her red eyes were a dead giveaway she was definitely crying. I got up and walked over to her.

"Baby, whatever it is, I'm sorry!"

She turned from me and covered her face with her hands. I held her.

"I'm sorry, baby! I'm so sorry. I swear I won't miss another doctor's appointment. I'm going to be there every step of the way throughout this pregnancy. I promise. I don't know what I was thinking earlier. It was just when you said don't worry about coming, I didn't think it was a big deal or it would bother you. I should have known better. Nothing comes before my family. I should have had my ass there."

She regained her composure and looked at me with heavy eyes.

"It's not that! You didn't do anything so stop apologizing. I told you it was okay if you missed the appointment today, nothing special was happening and I know how hard you've been trying. I know you would have been there if I didn't say not to come."

I was at a loss at that moment. I didn't know what was going on.

"What's wrong then?"

My mind went straight to thinking about the baby. I became fearful something was wrong with my child. She took a deep breath.

"The doctor told me I'm HIV positive."

"You are what?"

She burst out crying in pain and agony.

I continued, "What do you mean you are HIV positive? How the fuck, have you been cheating on me? Lia, what's really good? What the fuck is going on?"

"Marco, baby, I swear on the life of our child I haven't stepped out on you."

"You say it like it's so beneath you. You've stepped out on me before so why would now be any different."

"Baby, I swear. I'm just as clueless as you are. I don't know how this happened."

"Yeah I bet!"

Lia could tell how hurt I was. "I'm sorry. I know you don't want me now. I promise I'll get my stuff and go. I never meant to hurt you. I'm so sorry!"

She was hysterical. I hadn't had time to really process everything and analyze it. Because of my own anger, I missed the pain my wife was in. I wrapped my arms around her and gave her what she needed, my support.

"Baby, I love you. Nothing will ever change that. We will be together in sickness and in health until death do us part. I'm not going anywhere and neither are you."

"Baby, but I'm going to die. I have AIDS. I'm going to die. I'm dying right now, day by day."

It finally hit me what she said. HIV. Man, those are three scary letters. Did I have it too? Her crying intensified. I continued to hold her as well as kissed her on her forehead.

"I'm not giving up on you that easy so you don't give up either. We've been through worse things in life and have gotten through them. We'll get through this too. We'll get through this the only way we know how, together!"

I wiped away her tears. She looked at me and gently kissed my lips.

"I love you!"

"I love you too. We'll be alright. Watch, you'll see. We will be just fine."

For the first time that day, I was able to see her smile. I wish I was smiling inside as well. I wasn't though. I didn't believe a word of what I'd just told her except when I said "until death do us part." I knew I'd never leave her side but at the same time, I knew we wouldn't succeed where thousands, maybe millions, have failed and actually beat this disease. One thing was certain, if it was taking us, it was taking us together.

Chapter 7

I walked into the doctor's office, already knowing my fate. It would be a miracle if I wasn't infected but, deep down inside, I already knew I was. My doctor's visit was just a confirmation. I figured the sooner I had a definite "yes, Mr. Reid, you are HIV positive," the sooner we could move forward and find ways to treat it.

The initial shock of being positive started to finally wear off Lia. Every now and then she'd still freak out, but that was to be expected. It's not every day you find out you are infected with a deadly disease. That is life-altering news. You can't help but think about your life and how it will never be the same, after hearing those four words: "You are HIV positive."

The doctor walked into the office breaking my train of thought. He confirmed what I'd already known. He wanted to talk about possible strategies to fight the disease and specialists I should consider seeing versus him treating me, but he was speaking to deaf ears. I hard already heard all I needed to hear. I think a part of me wished it wasn't true. I wished I wasn't infected but with him confirming it, all the hope I had went out the door and down the street.

Everything seemed as if it was moving a hundred miles an hour. No matter how much I tried to prepare myself for the worse, the fact that I was actually positive really hit hard. The room seemed like it was spinning round and round. The lightheadedness started to enter. I needed to get out of there and get some fresh air. I needed time to just think. I got up and walked out of his office while he was in mid sentence.

I found the closest bar and parked myself there for hours, trying to drink my sorrows away. For once in my life I feared the unknown. I didn't know how people would react to me now. But what bothered me the most was I didn't know how to feel about my wife.

Was it really only one time she cheated on me? Was it fair to put the blame for her cheating squarely on my shoulders? Shit, I didn't even know if Lia had given me HIV or if it was the other way around. They say it can go undetected for up to ten years. Who is to say that I didn't have it before I met her?

Lord knows how much of a whore I was before I met her. The only thing I knew was that I was going to die from this disease. I didn't even know how I would but I knew what the end result would be.

I didn't want to die in pain or agony but knew I wasn't in control of my fate. I thought about Tom Hanks' character in the movie *Philadelphia*. How much he suffered. How much his family suffered. I would be damned if that was going to be me. I wasn't going out like that. I'd kill myself first before I put my family through what his went through. Hell no.

This was so scary because you never hear about any success stories of people with HIV. It was like I had no positive signs to look forward too. I mean, look at Eazy E and Arthur Ashe. One minute they were advertising to the world they were infected with HIV or AIDS and the next thing we hear is they are dead. It's like damn; he just told us he was infected.

The only positive example I could even think of was Magic Johnson and I still don't really believe he was ever infected. I mean he went public about being infected in 1991 and here it is over ten years later and he looks bigger now than he did during his playing days. They say that the disease is lying dormant within his body, but who knows.

What I did know is that I didn't have Magic Johnson money either and I'm sure he was paying out the ass for his meds.

There just weren't many indicators that living with HIV was a possibility unless you had money. I couldn't afford the drugs Magic or any other rich person could, and I doubted my insurance would cover the bulk of the cost either. Things just didn't look bright. I felt like Gary Coleman in a Yugo, SHORT.

The longer I sat there, the more depressed I became. My life wasn't supposed to be like this. I wasn't out there fucking women left and right. I loved my wife and was faithful to her. I'm not saying I was the best husband but I never cheated on her in the seven years we'd been together.

Even before I was with her, I really wasn't out having unprotected sex with a bunch of women. I mean I slipped up every now and then but that was mostly with the woman I called my girlfriend and not some random chick. I made it a point to make sure I wore a condom with all the others. In some cases, I made sure I wore two. I wasn't the type of man that would put himself at risk. I loved life too much.

My brother, on the other hand, would fuck anything that walked back in them days as long as they were female and knew how to say yes. I can remember as kids, not even the family dog would even go near him.

At twenty-two he already had two kids by two different women and another one on the way. A condom to him was like kryptonite. I hate to say it, but he was the more likely candidate instead of me. I'm not wishing anything on my brother. I just didn't understand. *Why me? Why did this have to happen to me?* I thought.

I fought back the tears that were forming in my eyes. I wasn't about to sit in the bar, in front of everyone there, and cry. I finished my drink quickly and left. I wasn't sure where I was going but I knew I had to go somewhere else. I decided to go to the one place where I could get at least some of the answers to the many questions I had.

***

I stormed into the house looking for Lia. I found her sitting on the couch in the living room, crying with the phone in her hand. At the sight of her in pain, I quickly forgot all about the anger that filled my heart when I first entered.

"Baby, what is wrong?"

"He didn't even deny it!" she said as the tears streamed down the side of her face.

I was lost.

"Who, baby? What are you talking about? What didn't they deny? Baby, what is going on?"

She ignored my questions.

"Baby, who didn't deny what? You aren't making any sense. What are you talking about?" I asked again, this time more sternly.

"Rashaad. I called him to ask if he had it or knew or anything. He didn't even deny it. He just sat there and laughed like everything was funny to him. He said I got what I deserved. I couldn't believe what I was hearing. He fucking knew he was positive and didn't even care. He said he wanted to teach me a lesson and that I bet I regretted ever leaving him now."

I walked over to her and hugged her, keeping my anger in check. She needed me, not my anger. She needed to feel some sort of comfort but more importantly know that no matter what I was here for her.

However, it still didn't stop my resentment toward Rashaad though. I wanted to wrap my hands tightly around his neck and choke the life out of his bitch ass. My mind was made. I was going to find him for sure. I just had to figure out a way to do it without Lia knowing. I didn't need her worrying about what I was going to do to him. She had enough to worry about and I wasn't going to add to the list.

"Baby, don't worry, everything will work itself out. It will all be all right. The universe goes around. He will get what he deserves. It will come back on him."

"No it won't, Marco. You always say that but everything will not be all right. I'm going to die from AIDS because my jackass ex-boyfriend wanted to get back at me for leaving him for my husband. Let's not forget, my husband is going to die because I got pissed off at him because I wasn't getting enough attention and couldn't keep my legs closed.

"I knew what I was doing was wrong and still did it anyway. Everything will not be fucking all right because everything is fucked up and it's fucked up because of me. I can't even blame him, because I'm the one who allowed him inside of me. I could have said no or stopped it, but I didn't. I'm the one to blame. I made my choice!"

Listening to her mention him being inside her stung. I'd already dealt with what had happened but hearing it, again, was something totally different. It was as if I could picture it. And though I was extremely upset with her for even stooping to those measures, I also couldn't help but shoulder some of the blame as well. All she'd ever wanted was for me to spend time with her. She didn't want another man. No, she wanted me but I was always too busy.

"Baby, we all make mistakes in life. You didn't do anything different than the next person. People cheat every day. I'm the one who pushed you into another man's arms. I'm just as much to blame as you are. If I spent more time with my wife or was as much into her as I was my job you wouldn't have felt lonely and unappreciated. You wouldn't have been vulnerable and wouldn't have given in to temptation."

"I know you are trying to make me feel good 'bout the situation but the bottom line is, I'm the one who opened her legs. I'm the one who said yes and I'm surely the one who didn't make his ass at least wear a condom since I was going to cheat."

No matter how much I tried to at least shoulder some of the blame, she wasn't going to allow me to and I wasn't going to sit there and argue with her. I knew what role I played and what my actions caused her to do. Yes, she could have done a lot of things differently but the bottom line was he knew he was HIV positive and he didn't care. He was to blame more than anyone in my book.

My anger was past its boiling point. That bastard intentionally gave my baby a deadly disease off of some get-back shit. Oh, he definitely was going to receive a visit from me. I could no longer keep my anger in check.

"That muthafucka," I yelled.

I got up and went to the telephone to call my brother. Lia snapped out of her self-pity.

"Who are you calling?" Lia asked.

I brushed her off.

"Nobody. Why don't you go upstairs and lay down, baby? I'm sure you could use a nap or something."

The phone just rang. I hung up and dialed another number.

"I'm carrying a child. I'm not the child and I'm not going anywhere, Marco, until you tell me who you are calling."

Finally, I heard the voice I was looking for answer the phone.

"Kenny, where you at?" I asked, ignoring Lia's question.

"Don't worry about all that right now," I shot back into the phone. "I'll get you updated on everything when I get there!" I said and then hung up.

"Marco, you aren't going anywhere!" Lia yelled as she grabbed my arm.

"Lia, move. I'll be back later. I have some things I have to take care of."

"What things? Why now all of a sudden do you have things to do? What are you going to do?"

I tried to act like I had no clue what she was talking about.

"Lee, I don't know what you are talking about. I'm about to chill with my brother for a few. I need to get this situation off my mind before I actually do something to that bitch-ass nigga. I just need to get out of this house and get some fresh air."

She wasn't buying it.

"I don't believe you."

"Lia, move now! I'm not playing with you. I'll be back later on. I promise I won't stay out too late," I pleaded. She held her ground and still didn't move. "Fine, I won't go anywhere then. Can I at least go in the kitchen and make me a sandwich or something? Sitting here arguing with you is making me hungry."

She moved to the side giving me just enough room to get around her and go into the kitchen. She was still in a perfect position to slide in my way, if I tried to make a quick dash for the front door. She was determined to make sure I stayed in the house.

I walked into the kitchen and opened the refrigerator. I wasn't actually hungry but I'd already jumped myself out there by saying so; I had to at least act the part. I closed the door and went toward the bathroom.

"Where are you going? I thought you were so hungry."

"I am. I did just walk in the house not too long ago. Is it alright with you if I go to the bathroom and pee? And even if that wasn't what I had to do, how about I wash my hands first before I cook? Is that alright with you?"

"Sure! It's not a problem at all," she said sarcastically.

"Don't get cute!"

She rolled her eyes at me and cracked a smile. I went into the bathroom and did what I'd said. After I finished using the bathroom, I washed my hands. Once I came out of the bathroom, to my surprise, I didn't see Lia anywhere. I heard her upstairs in the bathroom.

I paused and thought. A part of me wanted to join her and finish comforting her but I had a different agenda. My mind was made up. My anger was still at an uproar every time I even thought about the situation. Against my better judgment, I took my car keys out my pocket and made my way to the front door. My determination pulled me into the night air to handle my unfinished business.

Chapter 8

The sound of loud banging at the front door woke both of us out of our sleep. I knew it had to be something important for someone to be knocking on our door this early on a Sunday morning. I put on my robe and went downstairs.

I looked out the peephole and noticed two unfamiliar gentlemen standing there. One had on a dark blue suit and the other one had on a black one. I started to not even answer the door because I wasn't trying to deal with any Jehovah's Witnesses that morning. Then it him me, it wasn't a Saturday morning. That was usually when they'd find their way to your front door.

I opened the door intrigued as to whom they were and what the hell they wanted.

"Good morning, Mr. Reid. My name is Detective Benson and this is Detective Lawson. Can we talk to you for a second?" the officer in the dark blue suit asked. He had a skinny mustache and wore wire Coke-bottle glasses.

Detective? What kind of trouble is Kenny in now, I thought,

"Sure, come on in."

I showed them into the living room where they both sat down on the couch.

"Would either of you like a glass of water or some orange juice, maybe a cup of coffee?" I asked.

"No thank you. Is your wife available? We'd also like to speak with her," Detective Lawson asked.

That was alarming. Any other time I would have welcomed him being straight forward and to the point but not on that morning. I became defensive.

"Might I ask what all this is about first?"

"Sure, but we'd much rather explain everything while the both of you are present. We have no problem waiting while you get her," he replied.

Against my better judgment, I went upstairs and woke Lia up.

"Baby, we have company. Get up! The police are downstairs and want to talk to both of us. Lia, get your ass up," I said, rocking her back and forth trying to wake her.

"Marco, leave me alone. It's too early in the damn morning for this. I'm tired."

"Baby, I'm so serious right now. The police are downstairs in the living room and they want to talk to us. You have to get up!"

Finally it kicked in and she sat up.

"Police? What do they want with me? What time is it?"

"It's seven-forty-three and I don't have the slightest idea what the hell they want, but it must be something serious the way they are acting."

Lia got out of the bed and composed herself. She went into the bathroom and quickly brushed her teeth. Once she came out, she put on her robe, then followed me back downstairs.

"Good morning, gentlemen. I'm Mrs. Reid, how can I help either of you?"

I'm sure both detectives could tell neither of us liked the fact that we were being awakened early on a Sunday morning. Especially since we'd decided the night before to skip out on church. This was our planned lazy time and the only thing on the schedule was much needed rest.

"Good morning, Mrs. Reid. We are sorry to wake you this morning but we'd like to ask you and your husband a couple of questions regarding Rashaad Jenkins."

Lia looked at the detective puzzled. Why would he be here asking her questions about Rashaad, of all people? That probably was the question running through her mind.

"That is fine but I don't see what questions you could possibly have for me. We don't converse anymore and haven't for quite some time. You might be better served talking with his mother or someone who is a part of his life. I'm sure they'd be able to help you a lot better than I can."

"Mr. Jenkins was murdered," Detective Lawson replied.

"What? What do you mean he was murdered?" Lia replied.

Before either detective could reply, "What does his death have to do with my wife?" I shot out.

"Yes, Mrs. Reid. He was murdered," Detective Lawson replied ignoring me.

"You said you wanted to ask me some questions. How can I help you gentlemen," Lia asked genuinely.

"We were wondering what your relationship with him was exactly," Detective Lawson asked Lia, while looking me dead in my eyes, as if he were trying to tell me he knew everything.

I smirked.

"We don't have one. I didn't know the guy," I replied.

"Marco," Lia snapped.

Both detectives could tell I was agitated. It was written all over my face. Detective Lawson cracked a brief smile.

"I'm sorry, Lia, but he's asking you a question and all up in my face as if it's for me so I answered it. My mother always taught me to look at the person you are talking to, so I'd appreciate it if you have a question for my wife you look at her while asking and vice versa so there is no mis-understanding."

It was obvious the detectives already knew about my wife's affair and were trying to rub it in my face to get a reaction. Detective Lawson's eyes told the entire story. The only thing missing was why. Why would they have questions for her but yet trying to read me? Everything with cops is black and white, there is no gray area. You just have to open your eyes and see it. I was becoming nervous because I couldn't see their angle just yet.

"Rashaad and I used to date years ago, before I met my husband. Other than that there is no relationship between the two of us."

I was getting tired of this cat-and-mouse game. They weren't really saying anything to add light to the situation. I stood up.

"Gentlemen, if you have no more questions, please excuse us as we have a ton of things to do today," I lied.

The tension in the air was so thick it could have been cut with a knife. Detective Lawson realized he couldn't control the situation because Lia and I felt comfortable in our own home.

"Mr. Reid, it might actually be better if we finish this conversation at the station," Detective Lawson said, then paused. He turned to Lia. "Mrs. Reid, we are going to need you to come with us."

"Excuse you, that won't be necessary. WE can finish this conversation right here or YOU can be on your way back to the station ALONE."

The light finally went off. They knew about the affair, that we were HIV positive, and figured either Lia or myself had something to do with his murder.

"Marco, I don't have a problem with going."

I could tell Lia was still in the dark by everything.

"Lia, they think one of us killed him."

Lia looked at me puzzled. Finally the light switch was turned on.

She turned to Detective Lawson. "Oh my God, why would you even think that? I couldn't hurt anyone, let alone kill them."

"Mrs. Reid, if you had nothing to do with his murder, then you will have nothing to worry about. Either way, we need to finish this conversation at the station. We'll wait while you get dressed."

"What station house shall we meet you at? I'll make sure we are there with our lawyer," I said sternly. They needed to know that they weren't going to intimidate us in our home or later on at the police station.

"Mr. Reid, you are more than welcome to come down to the station with your lawyer. But we will be accompanying your wife there. We'll be outside waiting for you, Mrs. Reid."

I looked Detective Lawson dead in his eyes. "I have a better idea. How about you get in your car and radio ahead, letting your captain know that Kalia Robinson-Reid, daughter of Phillip Robinson, will be coming down to the station in about two hours. Don't forget to mention she will be with her husband and her lawyer. I'm pretty sure he won't have a problem with that."

Detective Benson instantly recognized the name, Phillip Robinson. He quickly interjected.

"That won't be necessary, Mr. Reid. We will see you both when you get to the station. You might want to bring separate counsel because we have a couple of questions for you as well," Detective Benson replied.

Detective Lawson quickly turned around and looked at his partner as if to ask, *what are you doing?* Unfortunately, there was nothing he could do. He was outranked and the decision had been made.

"We will see you there," I replied looking directly at Detective Lawson with a smile.

Chapter 9

The entire car ride to the station, I replayed the events that had happened at the house earlier over and over again in my mind. Though I knew what was being suspected of us, I was still missing something. There was a reason why fingers were being pointed our way but the how's and why's were avoiding me.

Once I pulled up to the station house I noticed our lawyer, Jackson, wasn't there yet. I wanted to wait in the car until he arrived but Lia refused.

"I don't have anything to hide, Marco. He'll be inside when he gets here. I'm not trying to be here a minute longer than I have to be. I just want to get this over with."

"Lia, we need to wait for Jackson. I don't want them trying to confuse you."

"Marco, how can you confuse the truth? I'll be fine, trust me," she said as she opened the car door to get out.

Against my better judgment, I followed behind her. Once we were inside, Lia walked up to the desk clerk.

"Can you let either Detective Lawson or Benson know that Kalia Reid and DeMarco Reid are here to see them?"

The desk clerk immediately announced our arrival. That was a bit troubling because it highlighted how serious the situation actually was. Murder wasn't anything new in our city, but it surely was in our lives. Neither of us had ever been arrested. This whole process was new. I was used to Kenny getting in trouble and having to bail him out but that was about it.

Detective Benson walked through the door and greeted Lia. "Hello, Mrs. Reid, we are ready for you. Would you please follow me?"

I stood up as well, letting him know that I'd be accompanying my wife as well. Detective Benson put his hand out, stopping me.

"Mr. Reid, you can wait here. Someone will be out in a minute to escort you back, once they are ready to begin your interview," he said with a devilish grin.

"That isn't a problem. My wife will just wait until our lawyer arrives," I replied, then sarcastically smiled back at him.

This was the second time they'd tried to speak to my wife without me present. I began to wonder if she was a target at all in their investigation or if I was. I didn't feel comfortable at all.

"It's your call, Mrs. Reid. If you'd like to wait for your lawyer, that is fine with us but either way, Mr. Reid, you'll be waiting right here until we have a need for you."

The door opened again and out walked a new face. The gentleman wasn't in uniform. He was wearing a pair of jeans and a blue polo shirt with a police emblem on it. He looked irritated. The expression that he wore on his face said today was his day off and he was pissed to be spending it in the office.

"Mr. Reid, we're ready for you. Would you please follow me?" the gentleman said. He then turned around and walked back toward the door.

"Marco, come on. Let's just get this over with. I really don't feel like waiting for Jackson."

"Baby, I don't like this. I don't like it one bit."

"I don't either, but neither one of us has anything to hide and we really don't have too much of a choice."

I agreed to go back with the other detective. We walked through the metal detectors to indicate we were clean and followed Detective Benson through a gray door. We walked down a long corridor. Offices lined the halls. I noticed Detective Lawson waiting by what I assumed was an interrogation room.

Detective Benson quickly went over to him and said something we couldn't hear. Lawson's facial expression showed how surprised he was.

"Mr. and Mrs. Reid, if you'd both have a seat in this room; we'll be right with you."

Now I was shocked. Detective Benson had been adamant about doing the interviews separately. What had changed so fast? I couldn't help but wonder if we were being treated like normal common criminals or if Lia was receiving special treatment because of who her father was. One thing was for certain: Mr. Robinson had more of an influence with the Washington, D.C. police department than I had ever imagined.

The door to the room opened again and both detectives Lawson and Benson entered. It was clear that both of them were finally on the same page. I started to get comfortable because it seemed as if we'd been here for a while. Detective Lawson turned on an audio recorder and began the interview.

"Mrs. Reid, can you explain to how you know Mr. Jenkins?"

"We used to date."

"How long ago was this?"

"We haven't dated in over six years. My husband and I were having problems in our relationship and we separated. That is when I met Rashaad. We dated for about six months, nothing really serious. Then, my husband and I decided to work things out. We have been together ever since."

"So you had an affair with Mr. Jenkins six years ago?" he asked for clarification.

"No, I wasn't married at the time. We ended up getting married after Rashaad and I broke up. We were only dating. We didn't get married until after things ended with Rashaad."

"I just want to make sure I have this right. You and Mr. Reid were broken up at the time you and Mr. Jenkins were together?"

"She already answered that question. She said we were having problems and weren't together when she met him," I said, interjecting.

Benson looked at me like he was disturbed by my interruption of the interview. I didn't care because I was disturbed by his repeated questions.

"Mr. Reid, I can conduct this interview either with or *without* your presence. The choice is yours." He then turned and looked at Lia, awaiting her answer.

"That is correct. Marco and I were not together when I met and started a relationship with Rashaad."

"So there was no point in time when you were with both men?"

Lia became defensive. "I don't really see how that is any of your damn business but, to answer your question, yes. I wasn't with both men sexually at the same time but I wanted to see if Marco really had changed like he professed before I actually took him back and stopped dealing with Rashaad."

Benson paused for a minute while he jotted down some notes.

"Did Mr. Jenkins know about the possibility of you getting back with Mr. Reid at the time or did he find out after you'd decided to go back?"

"I wasn't even sure if I was going back to Marco in the beginning so why would I tell Rashaad. There wasn't anything to tell him until I knew what I was going to do."

"You don't think he needed to know that you might be leaving him for your husband?"

"I don't see how any of this is relevant but, no, I didn't and still don't."

He rubbed the bottom of his chin with his fingertips.

"Hmmm, I see!"

Lia felt as though she needed to clear up her statement for them so they'd have a better understanding.

"I wasn't even sure if I was going to go back to Marco. When I knew he was who I wanted to be with, Rashaad was the first person to find out."

Detective Benson must have sensed Lia was becoming agitated.

"Would you like anything to drink? Maybe some water or tea?"

"No, I'm fine. I just want to get this over with as soon as possible."

"How about you, Mr. Reid, can I get you anything?"

I wasn't as pleasant.

"Sure, how about some answers to our questions. Does that sound like that is doable? Shit, I can get something to drink from my own refrigerator when I get home. Are we done? I've yet to hear you ask a question that explains why we are here. You could have asked all that at my house or better yet, over the damn phone."

A loud knock at the door interrupted us. The same gentleman who had said my services were needed as well entered the room.

"Can I speak with you?" he asked Detective Benson.

He agreed and left the room.

The gentleman looked at me and said, "I apologize for the inconvenience, Mr. Reid. I will only need him for a few minutes, then we can get ready to get you and your wife out of here."

I'd never been placed under arrest before or even in a situation similar to this, but I could tell he wasn't a stranger to dealing with an irate suspect. He knew how to handle the situation and any reaction I gave him or the detectives.

After five minutes, the door swung back open and this time the same gentleman entered the room again with Detective Benson walking behind him.

"Please excuse my manners, Mr. Reid. I never introduced myself. I'm Captain Reeves and I will be conducting your interview. Would you please come with me?"

"Are you through with my wife?"

"No, we aren't, but don't worry. Your lawyer is here now."

I guess I'd played that card enough by the way he threw his reply in my face. I knew I didn't have much of a choice in the matter. I gave Lia a kiss on her forehead and followed Captain Reeves out the door. I was hoping that wasn't going to be the last time I'd see her without having on an orange jumpsuit.

Jackson was right outside the door, talking on his cell phone.

"Hey, I'm about to go in now. I'll call you later and don't forget to file that brief in the morning," I overheard him saying. He extended his hand to me and I shook it.

"Thanks for coming down, Jackson. I still don't know what is going on but I do know my wife didn't do anything."

"DeMarco, you don't have to tell me that. I know she didn't. Let me take care of this so I can get the both of you out of here." He turned his attention to Captain Reeves. "Where are you taking my client?"

"We have some questions for Mr. Reid as well."

"He is represented by counsel," Jackson said.

"He isn't under arrest either. We just have some questions."

"I'll be fine, Jackson, just get in there with Lia," I said, cutting them off.

"I don't think that is wise. Let me just take care of Kalia first, then I can sit in on your interrogation."

"Jackson, I'll be fine. If I have doubt about anything, I'll then ask to wait for you," I said, trying to reassure him I'd be fine.

He tapped me on the shoulder consenting and went into the interrogation room with Lia to do his job.

Chapter 10

Jackson went into the interrogation room. For the first time, I finally felt relaxed. I knew he would take care of everything and straighten this whole mess out.

"Mr. Reid, if you'd follow me," Captain Reeves said.

We walked into a room that was adjacent to Lia's. I could see her, Jackson, and Detective Benson and Lawson continuing their interview. You always see the two-way mirrors on television but I never really thought they existed. The only thing different was we couldn't hear what they were saying. I thought that was the purpose of having one.

"Mr. Reid, you can have a seat," Captain Reeves said.

I did.

He continued, "Mr. Reid, I'd like for you to make an agreement with me. As long as you answer me honestly and don't try to bullshit me, I promise to not waste a second of your time with long drawn-out questions that really have nothing to do with anything. How does that sound?"

That was music to my ears. I didn't hesitate to agree.

"Deal!"

"Did you and Mr. Jenkins have any type of relationship?"

I frowned. "Relationship? You've got to be kidding me. I didn't have any type of relationship with that bastard."

"Are you sure about that?"

"I'm positive! I like pussy, always have and always will. Now granted I know he was one but still, not the kind for me."

"I take it you don't like him that much. Maybe you're even a little happy that he is dead," he asked, giving me enough rope to hang myself.

I didn't have anything to hide so I took his bait.

"Then you'd be right about that. I'm only sorry I wasn't the one who helped him meet his maker."

If he couldn't before, Captain Reeves definitely knew how serious I was at that point. He turned and glanced toward Lia's room.

"Damn. Don't you wish you could hear what was going on in there? I know I sure as hell do. It might help to paint a better picture," he said, smiling. He turned on a knob by the door that I hadn't noticed.

"When was the last time you saw Mr. Jenkins?" I heard Detective Benson ask my wife through the intercom.

"The last time I saw him was in January," she replied.

"January, huh? What was special about January? You and your husband were man and wife, why seek out a man who meant nothing to you?"

"I didn't go looking for him. I ran into him at a restaurant one day. My husband and I were supposed to meet for lunch but he got held up at work. Rashaad saw me and came over to say hello."

"How would you classify your marriage at the time?"

"I don't understand your question."

"And I'm not understanding the relevance, gentlemen," Jackson added.

"Were you and your husband going through any problems at the time?"

It was obvious what he was getting at. You could tell how much they indeed knew.

"Every relationship has problems and ours isn't any different but I love my husband. I loved him then just as much as I love him today and will continue to love him tomorrow."

"Is that so?"

"Yes. I know what you are getting at. I know what you are trying to portray and I won't let you. I love my husband. People are entitled to make mistakes."

"Alright, gentlemen, this interview is over," Jackson said.

Detective Benson laughed. "You know it's funny what people tape these days."

He pulled another audio recorder out of his pocket and hit play.

"Did you? Did you know? Did your ass know that you were HIV positive the night you fucked me?" Lia's voice said.

Then there was laughter.

A male's voice said, "Actually I have AIDS. I'm far from HIV, honey. You'll get there soon enough. Then you'll really understand."

"You bastard! Why? Why would you do that to me?"

"You really want to know?"

"I asked you, didn't I?"

"The same reason why you fucked me over when we were together. You knew all along you were going to go back to that nigga. You could have stopped me from falling in love with you by keeping it real with me from jump. But did you? No! You just strung my ass along, then dropped my ass when Superman wanted to fly back into the picture and save the fucking day.

"It really hurt me. I mean, it broke my spirit. No, you killed my spirit and now I feel like I've done the same thing to you. We are even!"

I couldn't believe what I was hearing. Even though it was a tape and was no longer alive, I was fuming inside. I could feel my anger spilling over my boiling point. The only comfort I had was that he was dead. I was glad that someone had rid the world of such trash. If you asked me, they deserved a medal of fucking honor.

"Turn it off. You've made your point. You know about my wife's affair but so what, that still doesn't change anything. She still didn't do anything," I said to Captain Reeves.

"Let's just listen to a little bit more. I get better," he replied.

"How the fuck can you even think about saying we are even? Even! I break up with you, you give me got damn AIDS and you call that shit even! How the hell is that even?"

"You fucked me and I fucked you. Yep, that's even in my book."

I looked at Lia's face as she sat there listening. I saw the same pain in her eyes that I'd seen that very night in our living room.

"You threaten my life and my family by giving me a deadly disease that has no known cure and you are going to sit there and try to say that it is the same as me breaking up with you. Fuck you! Fuck you! I have something for your ass.

If it's the last thing I do on this earth, I'll make sure your ass gets yours. You better believe that, bitch!"

He began laughing, this time harder than he did the first time.

"Wow, I never knew Mrs. Kalia Reid had it in her. Are you threatening my life, Mrs. Reid? That is funny. What do you think you can possibly do to me that is not already going to happen? News flash, dumb ass, I have AIDS. I'm already dying and I'm pretty sure it won't be pleasant. I have lesions now on my body the damn size of strawberries. It fucking hurts when I hold my dick to pee and that's IF I can even stand up and pee. And I'm supposed to be afraid of you threatening my life? Please, please kill me! You'd be doing me a damn favor. Go on. Send your husband. I don't give a shit. When I'm dead, buried, and stinking, guess what? You and that bitch-ass nigga will still be dying inside. I have all the pleasure I need in knowing that and nothing will EVER take that away!"

There was a long silence. I assumed that is when Lia hung up the phone and I walked into the house.

"Help me out here, Detective Benson, what part of that tape proves my client had anything to do with Mr. Jenkins' murder? I must have missed that part because nowhere on there did I hear her do anything but make a threat and vent her displeasure."

"Is that what you heard, counselor? Let me tell you what I heard. I heard a motive and soon it won't be long before we have more. After that, I'll be hearing the sound of a six-by-nine cell door closing after you client enters it for a long time."

"Now that was close to being amusing, detectives. Please make sure you notify us when complete you investigation and exonerate my client. Now, if you aren't charging her with anything, this interview is over and we will be leaving."

Detective Benson knew he was on the right track but he didn't have enough evidence linking her to the murder. Without that, he couldn't charge her with anything.

"We are done here. Have a good day, gentlemen," Jackson said as he started to get up.

"Jackson, wait, I need to clear something up."

"Kalia, you don't have to clear anything up," Jackson said, trying to keep her quiet. The fact of the matter was, he didn't know if she was guilty or innocent now but what he didn't know was she couldn't be charged. He didn't want her saying anything that would change that.

"I know I don't, but I want to. Yes, I had an affair with Rashaad but I never kept that a secret. I told the only person who needed to know and that was my husband. I didn't wait a week or two. No, I told him the minute he came home on the night it happened.

"Second, the reason why I called Rashaad was to see why he would do something like that to me and my family. I mean, my husband had nothing to do with anything that was between us. Now he is infected because of my dumbness and Rashaad's stupidity. Also, had he not been infected, I thought he needed to know that it was a possibility that now he was. Didn't he have that right?"

"Yeah, but when you found out that he knew and gave it to you on purpose, it must have pissed you off. Who wouldn't be pissed off by it?" Detective Benson added, trying to bait Lia into saying something she'd regret.

Lia fell for it. "You damn right I was pissed. I couldn't believe he would sit here and say something like that. I broke up with him. I didn't give him HIV. That is just sick and plain wrong. I could have killed his ass!"

"And that is what you did, right, Mrs. Reid? You killed him? Now, just tell us who you hired to do it for you and we'll make you a deal. You might even be eligible for parole in twenty years instead of dying in jail or with a needle in your arm."

"I didn't kill him or have anyone to kill him. The only thing I did was hang up the phone and start crying. I was devastated because no matter how much I wanted to blame Rashaad for everything, I had to place the blame squarely on my shoulders. I was the one who decided to have unprotected sex with him.

"If I was going to cheat, I could have at least made sure he wore a condom. I was the one to blame and now my husband has to pay the price for my mistakes. My baby has to suffer because of my actions. It would have been different if I was the only one affected by this but that isn't the case. Crying was all I could do at the time. I couldn't even move. I just cried with the phone in my hand until Marco finally came home."

Detective Benson cut her off; seeing a possible new avenue to pursue. "Then what?"

"Then nothing. Marco kept asking me what was wrong and all I kept saying was Rashaad didn't even deny it. He got upset and called his brother. Then he left."

"Where did he go?"

"I don't know. I kept asking him when he was trying to get his keys but he wouldn't tell me. He just said he needed to get out of the house so he could cool off. He was going to chill with his brother for a few."

"Come on, Mrs. Reid, you know your husband. How did you think he was going to react when he saw you were in the house crying? What did you think he was going to do? You knew what he was going to do. You knew he would find Mr. Jenkins and kill him for hurting you again."

"No, I didn't think that and my husband didn't kill anybody. If he was going to kill him, why not do it when we found out we were HIV positive or when I told him that I cheated on him with Rashaad? Why not do it then instead? I'll tell you why. Because my husband is harmless. He'd rather tell you a joke and make you laugh than fight or hurt you."

"That is enough, Kalia. You've cleared things up. Have a good day, detective. This interview is now over," Jackson said while helping Lia to her feet.

Detective Benson didn't have any choice but to let her leave. He still hadn't gotten anything substantial from Lia. I got up out of my seat and started to head for the door too. Captain Reeves jumped in my way.

"We aren't done yet. I forgot to ask you, where were you the night of the murder?"

"I think my wife already cleared that up but in case it's still a little cloudy, I went to find my brother and chill with him to take my mind off things. As a matter of fact, I got a damn ticket that night because I parked in a handicapped spot. Check your records. Now, my lawyer seems to think we are done here. Please excuse me."

Captain Reeves lost the smug looked his face wore. "You have all the answers, don't you, Mr. Reid? A word of advice, enjoy your time at home while you can. If it's the last thing I do, I will make sure your ass comes back through these doors. This time it will be in handcuffs and getting ready for a twenty-five-year stay."

"That sounds good to me but make sure Lisa Raye is my cellmate in your little dream. Oh, and if I even think you or any of your officers are harassing me and my family, Ill make sure my lawyer files a harassment suit against your whole department. You might want to think twice before you really decide to fuck with me."

"Is that a threat, Mr. Reid?"

"Of course not, I have the utmost respect for the law. It was just a piece of advice."

"Well, thank you for that piece of advice. I wonder if Mr. Jenkins fucked with you because we certainly know what happened to him. It's just too bad he isn't alive to tell us for himself, huh? Have a nice day, Mr. Reid."

He moved out of my way so I could exit the door.

"You do the same, Captain Reeves."

Chapter 11

Lia hadn't been herself for the past couple of days. I knew she was shook up by all that had happened at the police station. No matter how innocent she was, she just knew somehow the police would find a way to charge her with Rashaad's murder and then her whole world would come crashing down. No matter how much I tried to calm her nerves, nothing seemed to work.

When we first found out we were HIV positive, Lia made me promise not to tell a soul until we both agreed upon it. She wanted to keep everything between us. I wasn't sure what her reasoning for wanting to keep things between us was but I knew mine. I didn't want anyone's pity. I'd spent my whole life being the strong one for others and I wasn't going to have the roles changed. If I needed strength from anyone, I'd look toward my wife.

Being innocent never stopped people from being accused or convicted of crimes. Why should this time be any different? What made her circumstances any different than anyone else's?

In her mind it wasn't different. She anticipated the day the police would come knocking on our door to take her away. The stress of that and being HIV positive ate away at her spirit day after day. She quickly fell into a deep depression.

She started to talk about death. How she would die. What she'd have on at her funeral. It's like the minute she heard HIV positive, she automatically thought of death. I think everyone does that in the beginning because I certainly did. I also wondered how long I'd be alive. If I'd be blessed to enjoy a long happy life or if I'd be cursed with a miserable and painful dead. I got over it though. I had to. I wasn't sure how long I'd live my life, no one is. But one thing was for certain, I was going to live while I had life.

Lia was talking about what type of flowers she wanted at her funeral. Who she wanted to sing. What type of casket she wanted to be buried in. If it wasn't for her monthly check-up, I think she would have forgotten she was even pregnant. The baby was no longer important to her. It seemed as if nothing was important to her anymore. I hoped I was or I wouldn't stand a chance of helping her beat the depression.

Dr. Raderjah said depression was normal for people when they first find out they are infected. He said that over time they handle things better and realize that what they have is a disease and not a death sentence. He tried to fill us with all the success stories possible so we could see that there was such a thing as living with HIV and it wasn't a death sentence. Lia didn't want to hear it though.

Her depression was probably the best medicine for me. I was too busy trying to help her get over the depression to have time to feel sorry for myself. Her failure to appreciate life helped me to see how much we needed to. I began to live life again.

Lia walked into the house, tired from a long day at work. It didn't help that she was also battling a cold as well. She was the only person I knew who could catch a cold in the summertime but was fine all winter.

"Hey baby, how are you feeling?" I asked as I kissed her on the cheek, welcoming her home.

"I feel fine. How was your day?"

"I didn't do much of anything today. I went in for a couple of hours, then came home."

She fell out on the couch and curled up with a throw pillow. I sat down on the edge of the couch and started to massage her back. It really must have been a long day.

"Are they working my baby to death at that hospital?"

"Can we talk about something else?" she asked, seeming irritated.

I dismissed it the first time she tried to change the subject but I wasn't going to this time.

"What's wrong? Did something happen at work today?"

"Damn, you just can't leave shit alone," she shot at me, trying to get up.

I didn't move, making it harder for her to as well. It didn't stop her from continually trying though.

"I'm not sure what happened to get you this way, but you aren't going to take whatever it is out of me. I didn't do shit. I'm just trying to talk to you."

Finally, I moved so she could sit up.

"I know and I'm sorry. It's just… I'm so stupid." She leaned her head back and closed her eyes seeming like she was thinking. She paused, then continued, "I told Natalie."

I was lost. "Told her what? Baby, what are you talking about?"

"I told her I'm HIV positive. I felt like it was my job to say something. I mean, I work around patients every day, all day. Shouldn't someone know I have a damn disease I could possibly pass on to one of them?"

"How? By handing one of them a cup of water or some pills to take? It's not like you are operating on anyone. You are a damn nurse."

"I do more than just give patients their medicine. I put in IV's and draw blood. I do a lot," she said defensively.

"And you also have on gloves when you are doing it, don't you? You protect yourself from your patients just in case they have something they can pass along to you, right? So what is the difference? You are already protected. You didn't have to tell her shit. You wanted to."

She kept her head leaned back and eyes closed. I was pissed.

"I mean, how are you going to ask me not to say anything until *we* agree to then turn around and do the opposite of what you ask?"

"I'm sorry. I didn't think it would bother you since it was my idea to keep it between us."

"I agreed because I wanted to keep it between us as well. I don't need anyone trying to take pity on me. What exactly did you tell her?"

"I told her exactly what I said. I told her I was HIV positive and that since she is my supervisor and friend, she had the right to know."

I gave a fake laugh. "And?"

"And what?"

"And what did she say?"

"She didn't say anything. She just thanked me for telling her and that was it."

Now I was lost for sure. "So what is the problem?"

"This bitch went and started acting brand new on me. How are you going to be my girl one minute, then switch up on me?"

"What happened?"

"We have lunch every day. Well, I called her and asked what time did she want to meet up. She said she was going to work through lunch. I didn't think anything of it. I haven't been feeling well and really wasn't hungry anyway. So around two o'clock that afternoon, I started to get dizzy. I decided to get something from the cafeteria. This bitch was in here, laughing it up and eating her lunch.

"I smiled and tried to let it go. I expected more from her but I wasn't going to stoop to her level. I knew why she didn't want to have lunch. It was obvious. I knew that she really wasn't my friend like I thought she was. Then she saw me and instead of not saying anything or continuing her conversation, she rolls her eyes at me.

"I couldn't believe it so I went over and asked her if I could talk to her. She reluctantly agreed. We were out in the hallway talking. She was standing far away from me like I'm contagious or something ?"

"No she wasn't!"

"It wasn't like she made sure to stand thirty feet away but you know what I mean. I told her that her ignorance was obvious and for it to be coming from someone in management was absurd. How are you going to work in a hospital and still be so damn ignorant?

"At first, she tried to deny what I was talking about. Then I guess she felt like she didn't have to hide shit from me, after all, she is my supervisor. She asked me why didn't I just quit when I found out and said I was selfish to keep my disease concealed and put everyone else in jeopardy. She even had the nerve to call me inconsiderate.

"I was so mad my emotions got the best of me. I did what I had wanted to do the minute I walked into the cafeteria and she rolled her eyes at me. I punched her square in her nose."

I was shocked. I knew Lia wasn't anyone's punk but she was mostly all talk. Never would I have pictured her actually fighting someone, especially not swing first.

"Please tell me you didn't punch your boss in her face."

"I wasn't even thinking supervisor-employee but the second she picked herself up off the floor, she was. She didn't hesitate to fire me. I feel so stupid, baby. I mean, I knew I should have just kept my mouth shut and not said a word, but no, I just had to tell my *friend*. Now I'm jobless because of it."

I reached over and extended my arms, hugging her. It was time for the *"everything is going to be all right"* speech, but it had to be said in a different fashion.

"Baby, don't worry about work right now. I can manage the bills until you get back on your feet. Don't worry about Natalie either. Just be glad she showed you her true colors so you could see that she really wasn't your friend." I paused and laughed. "Shit, be glad she didn't call the police. We damn sure don't need that. They are already trying to find a way to put a damn murder on you."

"I know, right. I'm sure they would have been glad to charge me with something. My father wouldn't have been too thrilled though."

"Baby, seriously, because of our situation we have to be careful how we react to different situations. Not just for us but also our family."

She agreed.

"How are you?" My mind then ran to the baby.

"I'm fine. She did a lot of talking once people came over and separated us. She didn't really want to fight. It was all a part of her show. I guess she was a little embarrassed."

I felt relieved.

"What if she would have hit you in your stomach and you lost the baby? Did you forget you are pregnant?"

"Marco, I said I wasn't thinking. I just reacted. It's not like she wouldn't have been doing the baby a favor if she did."

"Excuse me?"

"Nothing."

I wasn't going to let her off the hook that easy.

"No, tell me. What is that supposed to mean?"

"Have you thought about the baby? Have you? I have. I think about the baby all the time and what my sick body is doing to it every day. If the baby is growing correctly, will it have any defects? Will it live to see the outside of my womb? There isn't a day that I don't think about my child, but have you?"

"Of course I think about *our* child," I reassured her. "I just don't like to think negative. I know what the statistics are. I was right there with you, when Dr. Raderjah explained them to us. But he also said he wasn't an expert on HIV pregnancies. That is why he referred us to an OB who was."

"So I guess you feel I think negative about everything, huh?"

I really didn't want to argue. I knew the path she was trying to go down would escalate into something I wasn't trying to venture into.

"Baby, I don't feel you think negative. I just mean that in a lot of situations you don't think positive. Yes, we are infected. Yes, the statistics say that we'll die from this disease but who won't die from something? I look at it like this, either I can sit back and feel sorry for myself, question why it happened to me, or I can just deal with it and live my life.

"Who is to say I won't die on my way to work in the morning? Who is to say that HIV or AIDS is going to kill me? You never know. We could mess around and beat this. No one knows anything but Christ so I'm going to let him handle what happens with my life. I just want you to do the same thing. Stop worrying about everything and just live life."

Chapter 12

I hoped Lia would start to live life more instead of worrying about and fearing death. For a while, it seemed like Lia had finally come around but it wasn't long before she slipped back into her depression. In a strange way, I was more affected by her depression than she was.

This wasn't the woman I had fallen in love with. She wasn't the woman I'd married. I could remember a time when she was so energetic and full of life. She was far from that at the present time. If there was such a thing as the dead walking, she'd be the prime example.

Thinking back made me miss those days more. I was determined to do whatever it took to get my wife back. She'd always been my sunshine on a cloudy day. The tide had just turned and now it was my time to be her sunshine on her cloudy day.

A light went off in my head. It was a little risky and would take some help to pull off but probably just what she needed. I started to plan a special surprise. I just hoped it would work.

"Special" didn't mean guaranteed and damn sure wasn't a synonym for "perfect," so I was taking every precaution possible. Dinner was a must and, of course, sex would be nice but she needed to be made love to again. She needed to remember what feeling loved felt like so she could appreciate it more and crave that feeling all the time. With her craving, she would have a renewed appreciation for life because she'd have something to live for.

Everything made perfectly clear sense to me. That was it. She needed to be made love to. She needed to be wined and dined. She needed to be appreciated. Her body needed to be caressed. She needed me and I damn sure needed her.

I went upstairs. Lia was out with her mother. Mrs. Robinson always had a way of cheering anyone up, no matter what the situation. Things probably would have been so much easier if Mrs. Robinson knew what was really wrong with Lia and why she was truly depressed. She'd know just how to turn everything around and show it to her in a positive light. We damn sure could have used the support group. It certainly would have erased our feelings of battling this disease on our own.

She couldn't know though. If we told her, Mr. Robinson would have to know and then we'd have to tell my mother and Kenny. Soon, everyone would know and we'd have to deal with the pity that would come with everyone knowing. Some probably more than others cause you'd be able to see it in their eyes. I feared that look. I could deal with the ignorance that would probably come along with it too, but the fear of people taking pity on me was something I knew I couldn't deal with. I didn't care to even try.

Lia was totally the opposite. She could deal with the pity because the support she needed also would come along with it. But the ignorance of people who really knew nothing about the disease but claimed they did would eat her alive. She would only be able to swallow but so much before she snapped. What had happened with Natalie was a prime example.

Nowadays when people hear that someone has HIV or AIDS, they automatically run for cover like the infected person has the plague. I want to just grab those people and be like "Hello, it's not like we have the Ebola virus or anything. The shit isn't airborne. It is okay if we are in a room together." That probably wouldn't do anything either.

I wish people took more time to understand things that they know nothing about before passing judgment. I've often wondered how I used to view infected people before I became one of them. It's kind of hard though, because I never had one-on-one interaction with anyone who was infected. I still don't think I would have acted like Natalie did. She'd been over our house many times. We even went to her family's reunion last summer. They were actually friends and not just co-workers. I guess she fooled us into believing she was really Lia's friend.

I walked past the room we were decorating for the baby and then I knew what the perfect surprise would be. I'd finish the baby's room myself. I was positive that it would bring a smile to her face. Hopefully she'd look forward to the baby being born instead of wondering if the baby was going to be infected. This seemed like the medicine she needed to cure her blues.

I called Mrs. Robinson so she'd know what I was planning and she could buy me a little more time to complete it. I didn't want them coming back early and the room not be finished or dinner not done.

Mrs. Robinson was more than happy to help. She decided to take Lia to a day spa. That gave me at least five hours to work with. Mrs. Robinson sure knew how to spend her husband's money. As the CEO of the largest private detective agency in the state, he had enough of it for her to spend. He didn't mind. He actually took pleasure in spoiling his girl. Shit, both his girls.

I couldn't blame him either. Seeing how Lia had him wrapped around her finger made me pray every day we were having a boy. I didn't want to be in the same boat as Mr. Robinson and damn sure couldn't afford it either. I'm sorry but my money isn't as long as his. It's not even in the same line. He is in the express lane and I'm over at the layaway counter.

I went to Home Depot to pick up a couple of cans of paint and what I needed to childproof the room. There really wasn't much work that needed to be done outside of the painting. I had about a good four hours left before Lia would be home so I wanted to spend it wisely.

The design of the room would take the longest. I wanted to put sky-blue clouds on the ceiling and the wall. Painting wasn't a problem but drawing wasn't my best ability. I got Kenny hip with my plan and he met me at my house. He was a genius with a pencil and some paper. I used to get on him about applying his God-given gifts but he never was trying to hear it.

He sketched out the outline of the design on the ceiling. I tried to think of a suitable design for the remainder of the room. Earlier I had painted the walls white to give it a clean glossy look. It finally hit me to do an assortment of designs for the four walls. I decided to have a boy cartoon theme on two walls of the room and a girl theme for the other two walls. Once we were sure what sex our baby was, Kenny could change the two misplaced walls to match whatever theme for the sex of the baby.

Kenny had no problem with it. He did a Spiderman meets Superman theme on one wall. Then a Spongebob Square Pants theme on the wall adjacent to it. For the background, he used the same sky blue I used for the ceiling for the Spongebob wall and a deep navy background for the Superman and Spiderman theme. He then used a purple background for the other two walls and went with a Dora the Explorer theme on one and a princess theme with Snow White, Ariel from *The Little Mermaid*, Sleeping Beauty, and Cinderella.

Once he finished, I surveyed the room and admired his masterpiece. I was in love with the room and hoped Lia would feel the same way. I was truly amazed at how talented Kenny was. Each wall looked as if the original artist had drawn the characters and not Kenny. Everyone said my gift to make people laugh was a talent but to me that was false. What Kenny had was a gift. He had a true talent. This was his calling.

While he was working on the room, I cooked up a storm. Dinner was the easiest component of the surprise. It was just a matter of putting it in the oven and taking it out once it was complete. I also made Kenny a little something on the side as payment for his hard work. He was happy with that.

Once dinner was finished, the only thing left to do was get the dining room table set up and to wash myself up as well. I was thinking of throwing on a suit to make the night more romantic but decided against it. I didn't want the hassle of getting out of it once the night's activities became more intimate. Once I got out of the shower, I threw on a pair of sweatpants and a T-shirt.

I did a last review of my surprise. The baby's room was set up perfectly. We'd already pretty much picked out all the furniture. The crib, the dressers, and the baby's changing table were all white, which pretty much matched the walls. I could have been a little more exotic with dinner. however. Though I made her favorite, I still wanted to do that extra effort.

I made Chicken Marinara which is nothing more than pasta, grilled chicken breast with parmesan cheese slices over top, and a nice marinara sauce. I also made a salad and some garlic bread to complement the meal.

I took out the good china and set up the dining room for a nice formal dinner for two. The vanilla-scented candles were burning, giving the room that nice-flavored smell. I threw on a Braxton Brothers jazz CD to enhance the mood. All that was missing was my beautiful wife to complete the ensemble.

I'd outdone myself for sure. After seeing all of this, she would definitely feel appreciated and see how much I loved her. She'd finally have a sense of how much she truly meant to me and hopefully a renewed feel for life.

I finally started to relax, knowing that I'd done something right. Usually my wife was the problem solver when it came to our relationship. I felt as though I was finally contributing to our relationship, emotionally.

The door opened and in walked Lia. She set her keys down on the hall table and picked up the mail like she always did when she first got home. She saw all our recent bills and noticed the letter addressed to her. Once she finished reading it, she looked around and noticed that all the lights were dimmed low and soft jazz was playing in the background.

Before she ever saw what awaited her, she had a smile on her face. All day she'd been pampered by strangers and for once, she was about to be pampered by the only one who mattered to her. She'd been so distant the past couple of weeks and thought she'd only pushed me away. My gesture only showed how much she hadn't, but rather how close I wanted us to grow together.

She tried to collect herself and headed toward the dining room. The smell of dinner filled her nose and only turned on her faucet of love more. I wasn't going to allow her to expedite the evening, even if she tried. This time, we were going to follow my instructions. I wanted her to enjoy every moment of everything I had planned.

She entered the candlelit dining room and saw how everything was elegantly placed throughout the room. White, long-stem roses filled a vase in the center of the table. The setting was perfect. The only thing that stuck out was my attire but she'd understand the reason behind it later if everything went according to plan.

"Baby, you didn't have to go through so much trouble for me," she said with a smile a mile long and panties as wet as the Atlantic Ocean.

"Trouble, what trouble? This is all for you so it wasn't any trouble but rather my pleasure. I think a lot of times you lose sight of how important you are to me and this dinner is like a reminder. I want you to know that you are the center of my world.

"I know you've been down lately with all that is going on and I could easily say things are going to get better but that I don't know. What I do know is that as long as we have each other we can survive and conquer anything. I strongly believe that. When you are down, I want to be who and what picks you back up."

She cut me off, "That is the thing, I don't know if I can be there for you like you are for me. I feel like this is all my fault. It's one thing to cheat but to do so without protection, what was I thinking? Every time I think back I just start to cry.

"I mean, no matter what you say or what you do, you didn't cheat. You damn sure didn't cheat with someone, unprotected. Yeah, you had your flaws and still do now, but you still stayed true and committed to me and our relationship. I can't say the same and that hurts me. I chose the easy way out and look where it's gotten me."

I could see she was starting to get emotional. I got up and hugged her.

"No, I need to get this off my chest," she said as she pushed me away.

"Baby, I want you to get it off your chest but it's not like you can't still talk while I'm comforting you. You want to take blame for your actions and that is fine but the bottom line is what led you to those actions. I'll tell you what, my actions did or should I say lack thereof. If I was the man I needed to be for you, then you wouldn't have had to go to another man for comfort."

"You can even look at that damn day. Had I not stood you up for lunch, you wouldn't have even talked to him. This is more my fault than it will ever be yours in my book. All I can do though is learn from it and treat you like the queen you are while I'm still on this earth. I'm not going to let HIV be a death sentence nor a punishment for me. I have too much to live for.

"I have too much life in me. I'm not going to give up on life and I don't want you too either because without you, I have no life. I don't have the same determination or drive. You are my motivating force. I can't lose that or I'll truly have lost everything."

She sighed in displeasure. No matter what I said or how I said it, she didn't share my perspective. She wanted the burden of her actions squarely on her shoulders. She only blamed herself and no matter what I said, she was determined not to acknowledge the part I played in our troubles.

"Baby, you know what? Let's not do this tonight. You went through all this trouble to create such a lovely atmosphere and here I am ruining it. Let's just enjoy dinner and each other's company," she said as she wiped away the leftover tears coming from her eyes.

"Boo, I don't want you to think you have to keep this to yourself. Like I said, I want you to get this off your chest if it will help," I reiterated.

"I know, baby, and I will but now isn't the time. Right now I'm hungry and all I want to do is eat and spend time with my man."

I knew we'd never get back around to talking about her dealing with being HIV positive but this was supposed to be a romantic dinner. How romantic would dinner actually be if I continued to push the subject? I decided the best thing would be to let it go.

***

Dinner was a little quiet in the beginning but, after a while, the tension finally broke. I was starting to have doubts about the evening, thinking I should have left things alone. Luckily for me, Lia was just hungry and that was the reason for her silence throughout dinner. She was too busy filling her stomach with food instead. I was happy though. I took it as a compliment to the chef and since that was me, it made everything even better.

We enjoyed a little wine while reminiscing about the good times when we didn't have bills and responsibilities. For once, she actually spoke positively about having the baby. She expressed how scared she was of being someone's mother but yet at the same time couldn't wait. The evening was turning out to be better than I'd even imagined or planned.

We danced. I'm not real big on dancing but my wife was. She always tried to get me to dance with her when we first got married. It's not that I didn't want to but I wasn't good at it. Actually, I sucked as a better analogy.

Yeah, I could fake like I could dance all I wanted, but if you got up close and personal with me, you'd realize I didn't know what I was doing. If my moves didn't give me away, your feet hurting like hell from me stepping all over them was a dead giveaway.

Once I sensed dinner was pretty much over, I went upstairs and ran a hot bath for her. Lia later followed behind me into our room and tried to sneak a preview of the setup I had for her. I stopped her right outside the bathroom door.

"What are you doing?" I asked.

"I'm trying to use the bathroom."

"Oh really? You must think I was born last night or something?"

She couldn't help but laugh.

"Well, miss, I wasn't so take your ass back downstairs and use the bathroom if you really have to go."

"It's not like I don't know what you are planning to do with the candles and the water running!"

"It's also not like I'm really trying to hide it either. Baby, what I really need you to do for me though is get a towel from out of the baby's room. I left it in there earlier."

"Here it is, I'm carrying a baby and I already have a grown-ass baby."

She left to go get my towel. If she was really paying attention, she would have noticed it was laying on the bed. I followed carefully behind her so I could see her face once she saw the finished room. She walked right in, looked for the towel on the crib, and walked right back out. She didn't pay the room any attention at all.

"Hey," she said startled when she noticed I was right behind her. She continued, "If you were going to follow me, you could have gotten it yourself. I didn't see it in there though."

"That is because you don't look for shit. It's right here!" I said as I turned on the lights in the room.

She covered her mouth with her hands in shock and disbelief.

"When did you do this? Oh my God! Baby, you shouldn't have. I can't believe you."

She hugged me and placed small gentle kisses all over my face.

"I take it you like it, huh?"

"No, I love it," she replied.

"I didn't know if we were having a boy or a girl so I gave the room a feel for both."

"Baby, I love it," she repeated.

She leaned in again and this time kissed me more passionately. The feel of her tongue rolling around in my mouth and her hands caressing my back had me lost within her touch. I wanted to rip all her clothes off and take her right then and there but I fought back the urge. Instead, I picked her up and took her back into the bedroom. I slowly undressed her and placed her in the tub. My plan was to pamper her. I was going to wash her body and hair but instead she insisted on me getting in the tub with her.

The sizzling hot water massaged our every muscle. While Lia sat in between my legs, I slowly massaged her neck and head. I wasn't a professional or anything but I wasn't a slouch either.

"Have you thought about any names for the baby yet?" I asked, breaking our silence.

"Honestly, it hadn't really hit me that we are having a baby until I saw that room. I can't believe you went through all that trouble. I swear I love you so much. Have you thought of any names?"

"I'm not real good with names so I don't know. It would be nice if it had some type of hidden spiritual meaning or something. You know something powerful. What would you say if I told you I wanted to quit my job?" I asked.

"I'd ask you why and what next," she replied.

"So you wouldn't be mad as long as I had a plan?"

"No, I'll support whatever you want to do. Where is this coming from? Are you thinking about quitting your job for real?"

"I won't lie, I have thought about it. I like my job but I don't love my job; there is a difference. I didn't think you'd support a career change though so I left it alone. Well, I didn't think you'd support what I was thinking about changing to."

"Baby, as long as it's legal, I'll support anything you want to do."

"That is what you say now."

"No, that is what I'm saying, period. Why all the fuss? What is it you want to do?"

I paused, wondering why I had ever opened my mouth to begin with. I should have just kept everything to myself. I was thinking crazy again.

"Baby, what is it?" she asked again.

"What if like I wanted to become a comedian? What would you think about that?"

She laughed. My feelings were crushed. I knew she wouldn't support the idea. Hell, I didn't like it myself. I mean, I'd love to be a comedian but it's not like I could feed my family off it.

"Baby, if that is what you wanted to do and you were serious, I'd be your number one fan, supporting you all the way. Is that serious what you want to do or were you playing?"

"Are you just saying that?"

"I'm serious."

"So you wouldn't mind?"

"Damn, what do I need to do in order for you to believe me? Do you want me to type your resignation letter to your firm when I get out of the tub? Will you believe me then?"

"Sweetie, I'm not saying that is what I wanted to do. I just wanted to know how you'd feel if that was what I wanted to do. Plus, how you going to type up anything for me? It would make sense for me to get some paying shows first, don't you think? Remember, I am the only one in this house working now, Mrs. Mike Tyson?"

"Ha ha, very funny! That is temporary. I'll find something at another hospital soon, trust me. I know it's just a matter of time. With every door the Lord closes, he opens up five more just like it or better."

"Excuse me, Miss Philosopher. Since when did you have such a positive attitude towards life?"

"Since I realized what a wonderful man I have in my life. You were right earlier. I do need to rely on you for help when I'm down. I really want to have this baby. That is all you've ever wanted and I want to be the one to give you that gift. Promise me one thing though. Promise me you'll always be in my corner no matter what though, Marco. Promise me you'll never leave my side. I know I can't do this alone."

I turned her around so she could see exactly how serious I was.

"Baby, I'm not going anywhere. Please believe me when I tell you this, I'll be your biggest supporter until the day I die and that isn't going to be for a long time. We are going to beat this thing and live long fruitful lives. I'm telling you we are."

I wiped the tears that started to trickle down her face and kissed her. My heart felt like a ten-ton brick had been removed. I knew I'd done good and right by my wife. That night wasn't going to be one of those nights where the surprise that was planned turned into a disaster because something happened to ruin it. It was going to be special. That night, she was going to learn to love again.

Chapter 13

Dinner was the perfect complement to the surprise of the finished baby's room. It also showed me how much work really needed to be done which I was happy to say was none. Once she stepped foot into that room, the only way she could envision herself was as a mother. After that day, you could even see a twinkle in her eyes whenever she, or anyone else, mentioned anything regarding the baby.

She wanted a little girl. I wouldn't have minded that myself if Mr. Robinson hadn't ruined that for me. I wanted a little boy who I could teach how to play football and how to ride his bike. Talk to him about girls and how to treat a lady. I wanted a son to carry on the Reid family name. I didn't want my father's name to stop with me but rather continue to live through my son and my son's children.

When we weren't talking about the baby, I made it a point to talk about life. I wanted her to finally see all that she had to live for. There was so much good she could do. With her medical background, she could actually learn more about the disease and try to organize a support group to help others. The possibilities were endless.

***

While she lay there in my arms she asked, "Baby, were you serious about becoming a comedian?"

"Why, would you have a problem if I was serious?" I replied.

"I told you I wouldn't. I just sensed you weren't playing and actually was trying to feel me out instead. I've always sensed you weren't happy with what you do but rather content. Is that how you feel? Do you feel like you have a job now or a career?"

"Baby, what's the difference? They are the same thing in my opinion."

"Not really. A job is something you do just to get by and make a living, but a career is something you want to do for the rest of your life."

I had never thought about it like that before.

"Why are you asking?" I asked, trying to buy time to come up with an answer to the original question.

"Because if you do feel like that, I want you to know you aren't alone. I've always felt that being a nurse was more than a good-paying job. As a child that was all I heard, 'You can't go wrong if you are a doctor or a lawyer' so I figured I couldn't go wrong with being a nurse. I could do that in the meantime but I never saw myself doing it forever."

This was all news to me. "Really, so what did you see yourself doing instead?"

"I didn't see anything instead. I never really had the 'what I want to be when I grow up' type ambitions. I always dreamed about having a husband and a family. I always wanted to be a good mother to my children. My parents spoiled me by showing me how a man and a woman are supposed to love each other so that was all I ever wanted. That is all that was important to me.

"It wasn't until my sophomore year in college that I decided to be a nurse and even then, I wasn't too sure about that. I've always been a people person and loved kids so I thought I could work in a pediatrics unit of a hospital and be cool. I never thought about what I wanted to do for the rest of my life. You still haven't answered my question though."

"Honestly, I'm no different than you except I started working at Bell Tech while I was in college and just never left. I enjoy my job and I honestly can see me retiring from Bell Tech."

"I don't believe you. I think you are settling instead of doing what you want to do. I can't remember but I don't think you started out as a marketing major in school. I don't think you switched until after you started working there. I can't remember though. What I do remember is that in school, your ass was hardly ever in class. You stayed in talent showcases telling jokes. That is why I actually do believe all this talk about quitting and doing comedy. It was like that was your passion, then all of a sudden you just stopped. I don't think you even had a major in school the more I think about it."

"I didn't have one at the time. I was still trying to find my way through school," I replied quickly.

Lia could tell I was keeping something from her.

"What is it?"

"What is what?" I replied.

"Marco, I know you. What are you not telling me?" she asked, making her question crystal clear.

"Okay, you are right about comedy. In high school all I ever wanted to be was a comedian. I loved Richard Pryor, Robin Harris, Redd Foxx, Bill Cosby, and Eddie Murphy. I'd actually study tapes of their act and how they would dazzle the crowd. I wanted to do better than all of them. I'd always practice my act in class. That is all I could see myself doing. Then my mother talked some sense into me and I knew that comedy wasn't going to pay my bills.

"It didn't hurt that you were so focused on your academics and I knew you wouldn't want to be with some clown who didn't have a good job and a degree to take care of you. I always saw how Mr. Robinson treated your mother and envied him. There wasn't any way I could compete with that man. He'd worked hard enough that he could buy either of you just about anything both of your hearts desired.

"He wasn't out chasing some childhood dream. No, he did what he had to do to take care of his family. I wanted to be able to do the same for you. I knew I was going to spend the rest of my life with you the first moment I saw you. Once I saw what you were accustomed to, I didn't want to drop the ball. I think I've done a good job at it. I also think it almost cost me my marriage as I came a little too much involved in work."

"Do you regret it?"

"What, providing for you? Hell no! I wouldn't change a thing."

"You know, people would always suggest that you should have become a comedian. You've always been able to make any and everyone laugh. And, whenever they'd ask you, I could always see a sort of resentment and pain in your eyes. I never understood why until now.

"Baby, I think you should do it. I think you should quit your job and follow your dream. I don't need my father, I need my husband. That is the man I married."

"Lia, you are crazy. I am the youngest director in the company and you want me to just throw all that away to follow some childhood dream. What sense does that make? I was only asking what you thought about me finding another job because it crossed my mind. I'd never quit though. I've accomplished too much."

"Marco, it makes perfectly good sense to me. You want to be happy so why won't you do the same?"

"I want you to be happy but I'm not asking you to do anything stupid either. Shit, how many people give back winning lottery tickets because the clerk put the wrong number on there by accident? I don't know any and, if I did, I'd damn sure take their tickets and smack them upside their heads with a thousand-dollar stack after I cashed it."

Lia cracked a smile. "See what I'm talking about? You aren't even trying to be funny but yet an ass and still it comes across as funny. I'm a true believer that we are all born with at least one God-given talent. It's nothing that we have to work at but rather it just comes natural to us. It's like when a writer picks up a pen and creates a best-selling novel with little effort at all. I think comedy is your talent and I would hate for you to ignore your true calling."

"What about you? What is your true calling or your God-given talent? Have you thought about that? If you had to choose, what would your career be?" I asked, trying to take her attention off me.

"Actually I haven't thought about it. I'd love to say that I know what I want to do but I don't. My dream for the longest time was to have a family."

"Well, you have a family now. What you don't have is a career. What do you want your career to be? If you want me to take your suggestion seriously, then I want you to do the same."

"That sounds to me like somebody is thinking about changing careers. What do you think?" she asked.

"I think it sounds more like someone better start thinking long and hard about what they really want to do with their life or I won't be doing anything. Now come over here and give me some more sugar. I'm not done with you yet," I said, grabbing her.

She tried to pull away.

"Stop, leave me alone, you jerk," she said playfully.

"I'll be your jerk alright. I have something right now that you can jerk inside you."

"Marco, that sounds so nasty! You can really spoil a moment."

"Are you serious?"

She didn't reply.

"That is what I thought. Now come over here and give me some sugar, sexy."

We started to kiss playfully at first until the heat started to rise. I continued to kiss her, enjoying the sensuality of her lips. The feel of their softness was enough to keep me content on any other night but not this one.

I continued to kiss her deeply and passionately. She grabbed the back of my head ad pulled me into her closer. I could feel the warmth from in between her legs inviting my manhood to come in for a tour.

I worked my way down to her neck and savored her sweetness. The perfume on her neck made for a bitter taste but the sight of her squirming as my tongue touched each different part of her aroused me.

I palmed one of her ample breasts while continuing to do a number on her neck. She had her eyes closed and seemed to be in a beautiful daze. That was all the motivation I needed to turn that enjoyment into pure satisfaction.

I worked my way from her neck down to her stomach, planting sensual kisses over her body along the way. I inched up her shirt with my thumbs until her bra was fully exposed. I stopped momentarily, admiring her perfect caramel complexion. I removed her shirt.

"Baby, turn over," I said.

She did. I undid her bra strap so only her back was showing. I opened the nightstand drawer and took out some green apple-flavored Liquid Love warming massage lotion. I had bought it at the Pleasure Place a couple of weeks prior. I'd purchased a few more toys I was eager to use that night as well.

I poured a good portion of it on her back and rubbed it in while massaging her muscles as well. I pictured her eyes closed, enjoying my touch and allowing the strength in my hands to soothe her ailing muscles.

I massaged her neck first, then her upper back, her shoulder blades, and her lower back. I took my time and allowed her to enjoy the full treatment. I'd occasionally take a quick break from massaging her only to taste the luscious apple-flavored oil by licking the small of her back up to her neck. I knew that was one of the easiest ways of getting her juices flowing, plus it was the perfect teaser for everything else I had in store.

With each taste, I'd blow on her skin first so she could get the full feeling of the oil as it heated with the touch of my cool breath grazing across it. Every time I would, she'd squirm due to the unanticipated excitement it would bring.

"Sit up, baby!" I said, licking my fingers free of all the excess oil. I actually did love the taste of the oil.

"Why did you stop?"

"I'm not done, baby. I promise. I want to give you a full body massage, so I need you to take your pants and underwear off."

"Are you sure that is all you want to give me? I know how your ass thinks."

"Then you should know that I have much more in store for you. Can you please do as I asked?"

Reluctantly, Lia did what I asked. I was glad she did and didn't put up a fight. I didn't want anything to ruin this evening. So far everything had gone just right. It would have only taken one argument to ruin it.

Once she had all her clothes off, she lay back down on her stomach like she was before. I had to pause and regroup before I went back to finish her massage because I wanted to just take her right then and there. The sight of her naked body had my dick crying to break loose of my pants and play with her buried treasure.

I poured more oil from the back of her right thigh down to her calf, then massaged it. Once I was done with her right leg, I did the same with her left. I went back and forth between her left and right leg until my hands finally became tired. They needed a break.

Lia realized I was done and asked, "Can you do my back a little bit more? It still hurts."

I knew it didn't but played along with her charade. I just wasn't going to be able to massage her back with my hands though. I had the perfect idea.

I reached back into my drawer to pull out my tool that would aid me with her massage. As I was preparing everything, Lia became a little skeptical of what I was doing.

"What are you doing?" she asked.

"Don't worry about it. Just lie down and enjoy your massage, boo."

"I would be if you were actually massaging my damn back!"

"Damn, give me a second, sweetie. I have this. I have to finish setting this up."

"Setting what up?" she asked, trying to turn around and see exactly what I was doing.

"Just trust me. You know I'm not going to do anything to you that would hurt, at least not yet," I said with a devilish grin.

I poured more of the oil on her back and then turned my contraption on. Lia jumped at the sound of it but quickly began to relax as it soothed her body better than my hands could. I continued to massage her back for another twenty-five minutes until she was completely satisfied.

When I stopped, I allowed her to see what I'd used. Even then she was still puzzled. All she saw was the massaging glove but the noise it was making confused her. I didn't tell her how I got it to vibrate the way I did.

I started to kiss in between her thighs, hoping to halt her search. She'd find what she was searching for soon enough but it was going to be when I wanted her to and on my terms. I stopped my kisses and began to work my tongue up her thigh.

The thought of me tasting her sweet nectar excited her. She eagerly anticipated my tongue inevitably meeting and playing with her clit. Though she was right, I also had something else in mind. Once I finally made my way up to the center of her wetness, I indulged myself with a fulfilling taste of her pussy.

As I eased my tongue in and out of her, I turned my secret contraption back on but this time on the lowest level. She couldn't hear it. I also removed the rubber glove I'd attached to it earlier. This massage didn't need any aid.

I sat it on her clit as I continued to make love to her with my tongue. She jumped when she first felt it but didn't question anything. The stimulating feeling was instantly overwhelming. She tightened her legs a bit but was in pure bliss soon after as she came.

I used that as my signal to increase the intensity. I turned it up to its highest level and worked my magic with my tongue. The regular smooth pace I went in and out of her ceased. It didn't matter that I was orally pleasing her.

I laid my contraption on her clit and got a finger grip under her thighs so I could take total control. I fucked her pussy with my tongue faster and harder. My oral quickly became lost in the sheets once she started getting into it and throwing her pussy back at me. I liked it. It actually turned me on more. I didn't need the aid any longer. I removed my tongue and started to profusely suck on her clit. The harder I sucked, the more she'd try to escape. My grip was firm by now so her attempts at attack didn't work. She wasn't going anywhere.

She was going to endure everything until I felt she couldn't take it a second longer and not a minute sooner. I continued to do it to push her over that edge. I kept going faster and harder causing her to come more and more.

She began to shake uncontrollably. That was when I knew my job was finally complete. My mission was close to being fulfilled. Once she regained control of her composure, she tried to recapture her breath. I rolled off of her and begun to wipe my mouth from her leftover juices. My beard was saturated.

We lay there, lost in the moment and mesmerized by the feeling of what had taken place. I glanced over and noticed she had already left me and was now dreaming. I moved in closer to her and placed her on my chest so we could cuddle.

I looked up at the ceiling and couldn't help but smile. That night I went to sleep happy and feeling as though I was on top of the world. For the first time in a long time, my wife lay on my chest fulfilled and satisfied but with something that was even more important to me, a smile. I was proud of my efforts. Even though I didn't come, it didn't matter. I was content with knowing she had. I was content with knowing that I'd made love to my wife and she felt loved by me.

Chapter 14

I rolled over and noticed I was lying in the bed by myself. I looked around trying to see if my wife was within eyesight, but she wasn't. I wiped away the sleep from my eyes and got out of bed to look for my love.

I walked down the steps and headed into the family room. There was no sight of her. I was puzzled. I knew she hadn't left. It was too late at night for her to go anywhere. I walked into the kitchen to see just how late it actually was and to make sure she really hadn't ventured off in the middle of the night. The digital clock on the microwave read 3:37a.m and her car keys were in plain view on the opposite countertop.

I headed back upstairs. I thought maybe my eyes were playing tricks on me and I had missed her shadow in the bathroom. Again, I was met with disappointment as she was nowhere in sight.

Where is she? I thought. Then it came to me. I walked into the baby's room and there she was staring out the window.

"Here you are," I said, startling her. "I'm sorry, baby. I didn't mean to scare you. I just didn't know where you were." I noticed the distraught look on her face. "Baby, what's wrong?"

She sniffled. "Are you happy?"

I was baffled by her question. I had just enjoyed a very passionate and fulfilling night with her. How couldn't I be happy? I walked up to her, placed my arms around her, and looked deep into her eyes.

"Are you kidding me? Of course I'm happy! How could you ask me such a thing? Everything I did tonight was to show you how much you mean to me and how important you are to me."

"I don't mean with me. I mean period. Are you happy with your life?"

"Baby, we talked about this earlier. For the most part I am. I mean, I can't really complain about anything. It's so easy for me to but I actually cherish my mistakes because if I hadn't made them, then I wouldn't be the man I am today. I'd be more flawed and further from perfection."

That brought a small smile to her face. "So you think you are close to perfection?"

"Hell NO! I'm light years away from it but I am closer than I was a year ago. Why? Because I learned from the mistakes I previously made."

"I wish I could think as positive about everything as you do. I'm not surprised though. I can't think of one time when you haven't made the best of any situation."

"Baby, I just don't see the point of sitting around and feeling sorry for myself or highlighting something negative."

"I'm not happy with my life, Marco. I try to act like I am but I'm really not. Earlier tonight, I wasn't totally honest with you. When I was a child, all I wanted to do was be a dancer. I love to dance. I'd lie in my bed and just dream about dancing on Broadway. Then as I got older I found my true passion. I watched an episode of *Matlock* and was hooked. I wanted to be the best damn defense attorney I could possibly be.

"My father was so happy and excited that I wanted to study law that he didn't really actually hear what side of the law I was planning on defending. By then he was already a legend at the station house, so he must have thought I wanted to be a prosecutor.

"In his mind, he'd lock them up and I'd send them away. It wasn't long before his dream became a nightmare. Once he caught wind that I wanted to be a defense attorney, that was all she wrote. He hated the fact that I wanted to set free the same people he was trying to put away.

"Baby, it got so bad, I just let it go. If I couldn't be a defense attorney, then I wasn't going to be anything. I wasn't going to be anyone's district attorney. I wasn't gong to be a tax lawyer or an entertainment lawyer. If

I wasn't a defense attorney, I wasn't going to do anything that had anything to do with the legal system at all."

I totally understood where she was coming from. Though I always tried to convince myself I made the right choice in choosing professions, I too wondered if I had made the correct decision by not following my heart. Listening to Lia earlier had me thinking. Comedy actually was the way I needed to go. It surely was where my heart was but it didn't make sense to change careers now. She turned away and began to start out the window.

"Baby, I think that is true for a lot of us. I act like I'm not bothered by my career choice but a lot of times it does haunt me. I think I could have been a damn good comic and sometimes find myself wishing I'd stood up to my own mother."

Lia turned around and looked at me. "Baby, what happened?"

"What happened? My mother is what happened. Oh, she wasn't having that! Comedy definitely wasn't a good way to make a living as far as she was concerned. I can hear her now, *'Being a class clown is not a job.'* She always had something smart to say about the subject. It didn't matter how I felt. But I tried hard not to let her negativity deter me. I actually did a couple of talent shows and won a few. I was also booed a few too."

I paused and shook my head reminiscing.

"What?" Lia asked.

"It's funny that you say I find the positive in everything. I remember when I was about eighteen, I'd been going down to The Laugh Factory trying to be part of the showcase for about three months straight. Finally, I talked the owner into letting me perform. I told him I'd do it for free. If I wasn't good he wouldn't have lost anything because I wasn't getting paid.

"Well, one night his headliner canceled on him. He finally decided to let me do my act. Guess who the headliner was? Martin Lawrence. He got sick or something and couldn't make it. Well, by then his show, *Martin*, was huge, so of course he had a nice size following. The place was packed that night. It didn't help that he was also a hometown guy too.

"I tried to pretend that it wasn't any different than any of the talent shows

I'd already done. I thought that would put things into a better perspective and help me with my nerves. Well, it didn't. In actuality, it was a lot different than a talent show. It was the first step at my career in comedy.

"I knew I was being blessed with the perfect opportunity. How many people can say they are a headliner for their first professional gig? I was pumped. I was ready to just wreak havoc on stage that night. I'd practiced my routine on my brother and a couple of his friends. I had them damn near in tears. You couldn't tell me shit back then. Oh no, not when it came down to the comedy game. I had the comedy game on lock as far as I was concerned.

"I don't know how but somehow my mother caught wind of my performance which still puzzles me, because I didn't even tell you let alone her. Of course, when they called me up on stage and I caught a glimpse of her in the audience, I froze. I was no good. I was off that stage just as quickly as I went up on it and never went back. If I couldn't perform in front of my mother, then comedy damn sure wasn't the arena for me."

"Why couldn't you perform in front of your mother?"

"I honestly don't know. I just couldn't. You know how when you learned how to ride your bike and you continued to constantly fall. You didn't get trying to learn though. Your father was right there, helping you get back on that bike and was right there until you learned.

"When I bombed on stage, my mother was so comforting. She was quick to tell me everything would be alright, but never once did she encourage me to get back on that stage. She never gave me the blessing I was looking for to continue to pursue my dream. She just left me fall off the bike and never put me back on it again."

"Then get it out of the garage," she said. "The bike isn't broken, nor is your will to learn, it seems. If you need help learning, let me be the one to help you get back on it."

"There you go. Baby, I often wonder if I made the right decision or not. I think I did. I'm happy with what I'm doing."

"Well, I'm not," she said in disagreement. "I never really looked forward to going to the hospital. I hated the fact that I worked with patients who were dying or have this disease or that ailment. After a while, it starts to play games with your mind. That is why they tell you to never get attached to any patients. Just as quickly as they are rolled into the emergency room is just as quickly they can be rolled to the morgue."

"Then why did you stay so long?"

"Tell me where I can find another job where I can work four days and then have three days off? Oh yeah and while I'm at work, I pretty much sit around and gossip. Did I mention that I still get paid close to fifty thousand a year to do all this? Where can I find another job like that?"

I had to agree. There weren't many, if any, jobs like that.

"So, in other words, you are in it for the money and not the happiness?"

"You've got that right. I'm in it for the money four days a week and I'll have my happiness at home with my husband the three days I'm off."

She then turned back away from me and started to stare out the window again. I could sense something was really bothering her.

"What's wrong, baby?"

She turned back around and stared me dead in the eyes so I could see how serious she was.

"I love you, Marco. You are the only bright spot I have in my life. I could tell you I want to be a garbage man and you'd support me. You support me in everything that I do. You always have and I know you always will. I just love you so much I don't think you truly understand."

As touched by her words as I was, I knew there was something more. What *"something"* was, she hadn't let on to.

"Baby, if you don't mind, I'd just like to be alone right now. It's nothing personal, but I just have a lot of things going through my mind. I want to sit here in my baby's room and just try to sort through these thoughts," she said.

I wanted to protest. I wanted to let her know that I was going to stay right there with her and help her get through whatever was bothering her. I wanted to tell her that the only way she'd feel better is to get whatever it was eating her up off her chest. I didn't want all the positive work I'd put in trying to rebuild her sense of life to go down the drain that quickly.

But against my better judgment, I did what she asked and gave her the space she needed.

"Okay, baby, but please don't stay up too late. You know I can't sleep right when you aren't next to me."

"I won't. Good night, sweetie," she said, then kissed me softly on the lips.

It pained me to turn around and walk toward that door, but I did just that. She turned back around and reentered the world she was in prior to me interrupting her. I stood at the door, looking at her for a good minute. Not once did she turn back around and notice me standing there staring at her. She didn't move or show any signs of being alive. She stood peacefully, looking out the window, lost battling the one thing I couldn't help or change, her mind.

Chapter 15

That night, I didn't get a good sleep at all. I kept waking up throughout the night. Lia never rejoined me in our bed. I've never been able to sleep comfortably without having her next to me. After the third time, I went to check up on her. I went into the baby's room and found her asleep on the floor. I didn't want to wake her to make her get in the bed so I tried to quietly pick her up.

She quickly awoke and protested. We went back and forth for the remainder of the night with me trying to put her in the bed and her protesting until I finally gave up. The final time I just put a pillow under her head and a blanket over top her so she'd be warm.

Afterward, I willed myself back into our bedroom and forced myself to fall asleep. I was thankful that I didn't have anything pressing on my schedule for the next day. I would have been a mess. I decided to sleep the next day away; at least that was my plan. Instead, I was rudely awakened hours later by the constant ringing of my telephone.

"Hello," I answered still groggy, but now irritated.

"Get the fuck out of bed and come bail my ass out!"

"Kenny, is that you?"

"Who the fuck else would it be?"

I sighed. "What's going on? Bail you out. What the hell happened?"

"Not over the phone, face to face. Get your ass down here and post my bail ASAP!"

"Okay, hold tight! I'm on my way."

"I don't think you are feelin' me. Fuck on your way! I need you here yesterday. I don't trust these muthafuckas. I have a feelin' they going to try to move me to county so go there first. Please don't make a fuss or my ass will be lost in the system fo' a couple mo' days fo' sure! Ya dig?"

"I'm on it. I'm leaving now."

We hung up the phone. I rushed and threw something on. I didn't know what my brother had got himself into but it had to be something serious and private if he didn't feel that Jackson needed to handle his bail.

***

Kenny was right. They had moved him to county. It seemed like I waited in the lobby forever after posting his bail. I'd been down there to get him before. I'd also gone with him to get one of his folks out on a couple of occasions. Things never took this long. Something was wrong about that picture.

Finally, I saw Kenny make his way out. I rose from my seat as Kenny walked right past me and straight out the door. The look on his face was enough to kill a man. I followed behind him. I didn't catch up with him until I reached my truck. I hit the unlock button on my keyless entry and we both got into the vehicle.

Silence awaited us. He hadn't said one word as to what was going on. I put on my seatbelt, turned on the car, and pulled out of the parking lot.

"Kenny, what the hell is going on?" I asked breaking the silence.

"You tell me," he replied.

"How the hell would I know? You are the one who called and asked me to bail you out. I was lying in my bed sleep, not in jail."

"You know what's funny to me? I'm standing on my block minding my business just like I do any other damn day and up pulls a black Caprice. I know it's an undercover so I really don't pay any attention to it. No cop would ever think folks on my block are that dumb enough not to recognize their whip so nothing was poppin' off from that point on. Plus, it wasn't like I had anything on me, anyway.

"Then these two square-ass niggas get out of the car. They call me by my first name and ask if they can talk to me. Now you know everyone on the block is starting to wonder how the fuck the fuzz knows me on a first-name basis and why they wanted to fucking rap to me. The only time they come around and call you out like that is if you snitching about something.

"I'm no snitch. I know there isn't a positive way to get out of it so I do the next best thing and decide to nut up on these assholes. I told the fuzz I didn't know who the fuck they were and unless they were a bitch who was suckin' and fuckin', I wasn't going nowhere. Luckily for me, one of them niggas got pissed and pulled out a badge. He told me I had two choices. Come peacefully or they'd force me to.

"I was as happy as R. Kelly at a junior high school prom because now niggas on the block could see I was being strong-armed and this wasn't a snitching-type situation. I tell them that I know my rights and I'm not going anywhere. That is when one of them stepped to me and as I tried to move back, they grabbed me and placed the cuffs on. They tried to say I was trying to evade.

"I'm thinking, what the fuck? You've got to be kidding me. I start to back up so I don't get my head rocked in case they got to acting funny and I'm trying to evade. At that point, I knew it was something serious. I just couldn't put my finger on what. I also knew that for them to make up a trumped charge, they didn't really have shit on me because they wouldn't have been asking me anything but instead hauling my ass away as soon as they stepped on the scene. They would have just told me how the story was going down after I was being processed.

"Finally I get to the station and this muthafucka asks me if I knew some Rashaad Jenkins. I'm like who? Fuck no, I don't know him. Then they tell me that they have an eyewitness that puts me on his block at least two hours before he died. So I'm like, what the fuck does that have to do with anything? I'm on a lot of people's block but that doesn't meant I murked them either.

"Then he sarcastically agrees with me but says is it common for me to end up on the same block of the man who fucked my brother's wife, the night he dies. I'm lost like shit. I'm thinking, fucked Marco's wife? What's really good?

"At this point I have no idea what the hell he is talking about. Then it hits me. I remembered you calling me one night pissed about some nigga who supposedly pulled a pistol out on you. Something about while you and Lia was out having drinks or some shit. I never thought your story made sense. Now I'm finding out all the real behind-the-scenes shit. So again, I'll ask you, what the fuck is going on? What kind of shit do you have my ass into?"

I pulled the car over and rested my head against the steering wheel.

"Kenny, my bad. I should have told you the truth from jump but Lia didn't want anyone to know about the affair."

"Don't trip off that. What is done is done. I need you to bring me up to speed though on what's really going on. Because if I remember correctly, when we went looking for that nigga, he was lost in the wind. There is no way they can put a charge on me. But what's bothering me is this nigga did end up dying, someone eventually caught up to him. If it wasn't me, I can't help but to ask who it was. Would you like to shed any light on that situation?"

"He was murdered, point blank."

"Yeah, I got that part, smart ass. Is the person who murdered him in the car with me right now?"

"You've got to be kidding me! I was with your ass that night. Did we find him? No! We sat out in front of his house and waited on him to come home for a good minute but did he? No! We decided to roll out and come back through another day when he'd least expect it. I'd love to take the credit on this one but his blood isn't on my hands."

"You sure?" he asked, as if he wasn't buying my story.

"I've said my piece and it's not going to change."

"Well you need to holla at your man Jackson and let him know what the deal is. They actually tried to get me to wear a wire and catch you telling me you did it. They were talking about they'd grant me immunity. That shit was funny. The fuck I need immunity for? I was going to kill the muthafucka had he came home, but God was looking after him that night."

"Kenny."

"What?"

"Someone still killed his ass that night; God couldn't have been looking after him too much."

"Oh yeah, good point."

We both started laughing.

***

Once I got back in the house, I went into the living room to ponder over everything Kenny and I had talked about. The cops were really after me. It wasn't Lia, but me. They were just using her as bait to try and trap me. When that didn't work, they went after Kenny and tried to do the same with him. This shit was really getting out of control. It would be only a matter of time before they started to put the pieces together and solve the puzzle. I couldn't let that happen. I wasn't going to let that happen.

"Baby, where did you go?" Lia asked, breaking up my thoughts.

"I had to go and get Kenny."

"What happened, his car broke down or something?"

"No, not quite. The police arrested him last night and I had to bail him out."

Lia started shaking her head in disparagement.

"When will that boy learn? He is too damn old to still be out there on that corner. As smart as he is, you'd think he'd realize that thug lifestyle isn't going to get him anywhere."

I wanted to just shake my head in agreement and leave it at that but I didn't want to lie. Kenny being arrested had nothing to do with him but rather everything to do with me. Against my better judgment, I did what I knew I shouldn't have.

"They went after him trying to get me. He was actually just minding his business, Lia."

Lia looked confused. "What do you mean to get at you? What are you talking about, Marco?"

I wiped my brow with the palm of my hand. "I wasn't exactly truthful about what took place that night."

"What night? Marco, what are you talking about?"

"The night you talked to Rashaad. I didn't just hang out with Kenny and have a few beers. When I finally met up with him, I told him that I had a situation. I told him that Rashaad pulled a pistol out on you and I while we were out at dinner, and we needed to handle it."

"You said what?"

"Lia let me finish. I told him that knowing it would get him mad enough to go look for Rashaad without having to tell him the truth. The police took care of that though. They told him you had an affair."

"What? Does he know we are HIV positive?"

"If he does, he didn't let on to it. I don't think he does though. He didn't say anything about that and he would have brought it up if he knew."

"Did you kill him, Marco?"

"No, I swear I didn't. We stayed parked out front of his house for a good two hours waiting for him to come home, but he never did. I just figured he knew that I would be after his ass. I told Kenny to get out of there and we'd come back another time.

"He went back to his place. I got in my car and came home. After that, I saw it was pointless to even do anything to him. If anything, I'd just be doing him a favor by putting him out of his misery. I wasn't going to do that. I wanted that bastard to suffer."

Lia looked at me as if she didn't know what to say. Even if she did, she couldn't find the words to articulate her thoughts. I knew I'd gotten myself in a huge mess. The cops already had a motive but now they could place me at the scene too. The only thing keeping my black ass out of jail was that Rashaad was alive when witnesses saw us.

She got up from the couch and headed out the room. Though I told her more than I wanted to, I didn't tell her the most important thing. I found a way to lie and keep the fact that I knew exactly who had killed Rashaad to myself. That, I planned on taking to my grave.

Chapter 16

I spent the better part of the morning buried under paperwork. As usual, the higher executive's brainstorm and came up with a plant to increase our customer base. Well, brainstorming for them means, *'Hey we need more customers.' 'I agree.' 'Put it on Reid's desk and tell him to connect the dots.'* They left me nothing but a pile of nothing to magically turn into something. I don't know what upset me the most: the fact that I had to do all the work by myself; or they'd take the credit for the finished product after I'd put in all the long hours to bring it to life.

I'd been working feverishly trying to figure out the best way to increase our subscriber base without having Finance come down my back. I would be increasing our expenses during the process. I needed something to take my mind off the stress so I called Lia.

I tried to make it a rule never to bring work home but this was one of those rare exceptions. My back was up against the wall and the pressure was on. Most of the time, Lid didn't mind since I was at home with her rather than at the office. It made things a lot easier between us because if I needed to take a break and spend a little time with her I could. I'd just go back and finish working after she fell asleep.

"Hello," Lia answered the phone.

"Hey sweetie, what are you doing?"

"Nothing, I'm just getting ready. Are you going to meet me there or are you picking us up?"

Shit! I thought. I totally had forgotten all about our monthly OB check-up appointment. Those damn things just snuck up on you.

Letting her know I forgot was definitely out of the question so I played along.

"I was planning on meeting you there. Why? Did you need me to pick you up? Is something wrong?"

"No, I wasn't sure and didn't want you to come get me and I'm not even here. Well, don't forget it's at one p.m. Please don't be late. I have an interview at three-thirty and I'm not trying to be late and miss it."

I was caught off guard a bit. This was the first I'd heard about this job interview. She was usually good about keeping me informed about things like that. She loved for me to wish her luck or prep her for the interview the night before. I wanted to go into more detail, about the situation, but I didn't have time to further investigate.

I needed to try to cram in as much work as possible while I had a little bit of time. I surely was going to have a long night catching up and still trying to finish all that needed to be done.

"I'll be there, baby. I promise I won't be late," I replied.

It didn't dawn on me until after we'd hung up that she'd said "us" referring to her and the baby. My smile could have lit my entire office building and the one across the street.

Finally the breakthrough I'd been looking for. She finally showed some sort of sign that she was looking forward to having the baby. Before, she wouldn't even acknowledge the fact that she was pregnant. It was finally evident that slowly but surely her depression was subsiding and she was starting to embrace the idea of becoming a parent. I was way past that point but looked forward to catching Lia up with me.

***

I got to the doctor's office a little before 12:45. I didn't see Lia anywhere but didn't panic either. I knew she'd be there within the next couple of minutes if she was running late. The door leading to the examining rooms opened and Lia came out. I stood up and met her halfway with a kiss to her cheek.

"Hey baby. How long have you been here?"

"I just got here. Don't worry, you aren't late, Marco. I came in a little early because I wanted to make sure I get out of here early enough to make it to my interview."

Lia gave me exactly what I needed. Earlier I didn't try to find out more about the interview because I didn't have the time. I didn't want to bring it back up as if it were an issue but didn't have to now that she'd opened that door for me.

"So tell me about this job."

"What job?"

"The job you applied for. You know...the one you are interviewing for in a couple of hours."

"Oh, I'm not interviewing for a job. It's for school. I decided to follow my dream. I'm going to become a defense attorney. The program I'm trying to get into requires you send in an essay explaining why you want to be a part of it and why you should be accepted."

"Are you serious? That is out of sight, baby. Why didn't you tell me? Why am I just hearing about this now? You know I'm your biggest fan."

She shook her head and motioned her arms as to say *I don't know*. This was her moment and she didn't need me getting on her about why she didn't talk to me earlier. The fact was she was talking to me now so I needed to concentrate more on that than anything else.

"I'm really praying that I get in. Every year they have over ten-thousand applicants and only select the top forty for interviews."

I cut her off. "How many slots do they have available for the program?"

"Ten. I have a twenty-five percent chance of being selected."

I could tell she was a little dejected. I didn't want her to give up her hope before she even interviewed. Confidence is everything and if she conveyed a lack of it, I'm sure it would have been a huge turn-off.

"Baby, forget the odds. You've already exceeded them. Listen to what you said. Out of ten-thousand applicants, only forty are selected for interviews. That means you only had a four percent chance of getting an interview and here you are getting that today so your chances have done nothing but improve in my eyes. The way I see it, the hard part is already over."

"You are right but I don't think I could take them telling me no after meeting me. It would have been so much easier to get turned down because of my essay. Then, I could say they didn't know what they were passing on. But now, it's like *I'm sorry, your personality isn't good enough to get into our program. Thank you but no thank you.*

"Baby, a fifteen- or thirty-minute interview isn't getting to know you. I could see if they spent a week with you or something like that, but not thirty minutes to an hour. What did they really get to know? Shit, even if they spent a week with you, they still wouldn't know the real you, only their perception of you.

"I'm sorry but you are reading too much into it. They are going to ask you some questions and you are going to answer them. If your answers don't fit into their scheme of things, then they'll go with someone else. That isn't a knock against you or your personality, boo.

"It's their loss. You are still going to get your degree. You are still going to become a defense attorney whether I have to pay for it or an institution does. Just relax and be yourself. If you do that, trust me you'll be fine and they'll love you as much as we all do."

I shocked myself with that one. That was a damn good pep talk. If I was in her shoes, I would have been pumped up and ready to take on the world. I pretty much guaranteed she'd be able to live out her dream of being a defense attorney. She'd be able to have her career instead of just working another job. How many times in life can you say you are in a win-win situation? Usually, it's the other way around.

"Mrs. Reid," the nurse called through the open door.

We both stood up to go back to the examining room.

Lia looked at me and cracked a smile. "I guess you are right."

"Shit, who do you think you are fooling? I know I am right. Watch, you'll see!"

***

I was going out of my mind with excitement, knowing that Lia was planning for a future. The step she was taking to achieve her career was all the evidence I needed. Things seemed real bleak when she first found out she was HIV positive but now she was continuing to live her life to the fullest.

I'd spoken to just about every doctor possible about her and all of them pretty much said she'd come around sooner or later. It just took time for her to adjust. I'm glad they were right because I was really worried for a while she'd never break out of her depression.

When we first found out we were infected, we both decided to join a support group with other infected people. The doctors thought it would be a good way to help us cope. Instead of them having to give us medical answers to all our questions, why not interact with people who were living with the disease and see what worked best with them? There was no better support than real-life testimony, from real live people. The phrase "Living with HIV" was an actual way of life and not a myth.

At first, I didn't think I'd really need the group, but the more sessions I participated in it became more apparent that I did. Thought I'd never allow Lia to see it, I had my doubts also. There were times when negativity clouded my mind and I couldn't tell which way as up or down but my support group helped me put things into perspective.

Until that moment in the waiting room, I never really realized how much the group was helping Lia also. Not only was she looking forward to the baby, but she was trying to have a career. You have to be alive and kicking to have that so death was no longer her concern. That allowed me to breathe easy, or so I thought.

We followed the nursing assistant back to the examining room and awaited the doctor. This was our second examination in this office, so we were still getting used to the regular routine. Lia would go use the bathroom in a cup. Supposedly it was to test for any infections or blood sugar problems. After that she'd have her blood pressure taken and get weighed.

It amazed me how women usually complained about gaining weight in a normal situation but when it came to pregnancy, they gain weight according to a schedule. Everything was fine then and the perfect excuse would be *"It was the baby"* or *"I'm on eating like this because I'm pregnant."* The second they leave the hospital after delivery, they are back to complaining about their weight again. *"Look at how much weight I gained"* or the question every man hates to hear, *"Baby, do you think I'm fat?"*

As we made our way down the corridor, I admired all the pictures strategically hung on the wall. I hadn't noticed them the first time we were there. All the pictures were of either newborn babies or children smiling. Two of them stood out to me though. There was a picture of a woman holding her newborn with a tear of joy sliding down her cheek. She was trying to hand the baby to a man, presumably its father. The other was a picture of a couple in a hospital bed together with the newborn close by. All of them were sleeping.

I couldn't help but envision that being my family. I could see Lia in that hospital robe, exhausted from pushing our child through her birth canal and me, basking in the excitement of being a father. I could see us in that same hospital bed cuddling one another while we slept. That was my family in those pictures and what made it even better, was the sign that read "Families Living with HIV" on both pictures.

"Ms. Reid, if you'd get undressed for us and put on that robe, the doctor will be in shortly," the nurse said as she opened the door to the examining room for us.

"Okay."

In any other situation, watching Lia take her clothes off would have been a no-no if she didn't want to have some sort of fun. The only time she'd get a pass is if it was that time of the month. Even then it better not be close to the last day because it still might be on. That was a problem I didn't have to worry about for the next five to six months.

I stood up and walked toward her as she laid her slacks down and was removing her top. She was startled when she saw me right in front of her, once her top was over her head.

"Boy, what are you doing?"

"I'm trying to play a little doctor," I said, wrapping my arms around her and pulling her closer to me.

I started to kiss her gently on her neck and worked my tongue across it. "Marco, what are you doing?" she said as if she was becoming weak.

She wrapped both her arms around my neck and started rubbing the top of my head with her right hand. That was a dead giveaway that she was into it and game for anything. I cupped her right breast and started to massage her nipple through her bra with my index finger and thumb. She started to squirm passionately as the heat begun to creep through her veins.

She propped her left leg up on the table, exposing her smooth caramel complexioned thigh. I took my hand off her breast and ran it up and down her thigh. Every time I'd move my hand up, I could feel the warmth trying to escape from her panties. I took my tongue and worked it up her neck, across her lips, and into her mouth.

She moved her body closer to the examining table to lie down and I followed her. Our tongues never broke their lock on one another but continued to erotically wrestle back and forth, each not trying to give an inch to the other one.

"Stop, baby! Stop!" she said, trying to catch her breath as she broke our kiss and pushed me back. "Dr. Norton will be in here in a minute."

I didn't think she'd be so inviting and we'd get so far into it so I was past my point of no return. I didn't care who saw us. He knew we were having sex. She was pregnant.

"Baby, I'm not thinking about the doctor right now. You started something and I'm damn sure going to finish it."

I wanted to lock the door and give us the privacy we needed. I didn't know what our explanation would be for why it was locked and damn sure didn't care. The large bulge trying to escape my pants was evidence enough. But luck wasn't on my side that day. My desires would have to wait. As I moved toward the door to lock it, Dr. Norton walked in the room.

Thankfully for him, he was reading something in Lia's medical chart as he walked in. Had he not been, he would have seen my bedroom soldier aimed squarely at him and the jig would have been up. I had a new meaning for the phrase *rock hard*. By the time he looked up, which was only but a few seconds later, the threat was gone. My soldier was no longer standing at attention.

Lia grabbed the gown and tried to cover herself up since she was lying there in her bra and panties.

"Oh I'm sorry, Ms. Reid," Dr. Norton apologized.

"It's no problem. I got caught up talking to my husband about something," she quickly replied.

She was talking to me about something alright but it was in the language of love. He turned around while she finished putting the medical gown on.

"That is quite all right. I should have knocked prior to entering the room anyway. I do apologize. I do have good news for you. We received your HBV test results and everything looks fine."

Lia cut him off, "it's alright for you to turn around now."

He put the chart down on the counter top, went to the sink, and washed his hands.

"So how is your day today?" he asked.

"Today has been a wonderful day. It would be even better if my husband was having this baby for me," Lia replied jokingly.

I cracked a smile.

Dr. Norton was alright. We decided to take Dr. DeSandes' advice and find an obstetrician who specialized in dealing with HIV-positive mothers. My first request was for a black one. Why? I hadn't a clue but when Dr. DeSandes assured us that Dr. Norton was not black, however, he was one of the best in his profession on the Atlantic Coast, black was no longer a priority.

I wanted to have a healthy baby and a healthy wife. The best sounded like the right way to go to me instead of wanting someone of a certain color. He or she could have been green or purple for all I cared. My family's health was the only thing that mattered to me.

Dr. Norton grabbed the cart with what looked like a micro EKG machine on it. The reason why I knew it wasn't an EKG machine, was because Lia didn't have heart trouble. It also didn't have long straps with the patches you put on your chest. Instead, it had what looked like a mini-microphone.

"Go ahead and lie down for me, Mrs. Reid," Dr. Norton said as he was bringing the cart closer to the examining table.

I was puzzled because this was the first time I had seen this being done. The first time we came in, we'd arrived nearly forty-five minutes late. We got lost trying to find the place so he pretty much rushed through everything.

He pulled out a tube of KY Jelly, opened her robe so it only exposed her stomach, and squirted some lubricant on her stomach. Had this been a different type situation, I wouldn't have been so interested in a strange man putting KY Jelly on my wife's stomach. Instead, someone would have been pulling me off of him because I would have been trying to kill his ass for sure.

He grabbed the device that resembled a mini-microphone and he put it on Lia's stomach. I didn't even notice when he turned the machine on. All you could hear was air. I began to wonder if something was wrong with the baby or if another disaster was about to enter our lives. He continued to move it around her stomach until I heard the words that brought instant joy to my life.

"This is your baby's heartbeat."

You couldn't tell me shit at that moment. Someone could have entered the room and told me my car had been stolen, I was fired from my job, and our house had burned down and I wouldn't have heard one word they said. I would have had the same smile on my face, lost in amazement at the sound of the constant beating which indicated the life of my child; our child.

I looked up at Lia and noticed a tear forming in her eye. The look on her face spoke volumes. If I ever doubted how much she wanted to have the baby, I no longer did at that point. She was oozing with excitement and it was written all over her face.

***

Once Lia got dressed, we headed for Dr. Norton's office. He was sitting at his desk writing notes down in Lia's medical chart. According to him everything looked pretty good and there were no indications of complications with Lia's pregnancy. That was a huge relief.

My main concern was the health of our baby. For the longest time, no one would ever tell us to a certainty if the baby would contract HIV as well. I made it a point to get some answers from Dr. Norton to the question during this visit.

"Dr. Norton, do you mind if I ask you a few questions?" I asked.

"Sure, how can I help you?"

"Well, my main concern is the baby. Will he contract the disease too since both of us are infected? I must admit that I'm very ignorant when it comes to this whole situation. To me, it seems like the baby would definitely have the disease since both of us do, but I've been hearing from other sources that isn't totally true. Is that true? I mean, what are his chances of not getting it?"

"First, let me say, Mr. Reid, I don't think that is an ignorant question at all. I think it's a very good question and unless you really study HIV pregnancies, how would you know the answer to that?" He paused, and then continued. "To answer your question, an HIV-positive pregnant woman, provided that she does not take any anti-HIV medication, has a twenty-five percent chance of passing HIV to her baby."

I cut him off.

"Are you sure? Only a twenty-five percent chance? I mean, you'd think it would be much higher. So you mean if my baby doesn't take any HIV medications at all, there is still a seventy-five percent chance our child won't have HIV?"

"That is correct."

"What are the chances he'll get it if she does take the medication?"

"If she takes anti-HIV drug therapy while she is pregnant, the risk of her passing the virus to her baby is much lower, in some cases as low as two percent."

My facial expression said it all. There was probably a two percent chance I could cross the street and be hit by a damn bus. I didn't need to hear any more. I was all set.

"I'm confused, because I read on the internet that all babies born to HIV-infected mothers test positive for the virus," Lia interjected.

"That is correct, they do. It is important to keep in mind what the HIV test is. These tests look for antibodies to HIV. They do not look for the virus itself. Because a fetus is exposed to his or her mother's HIV antibodies, he or she will automatically test positive after birth. These antibodies can remain in the baby's body for more than eighteen months after he or she is born.

"Most hospitals now test babies born to HIV-infected women using PCR. This test can be performed within a few days after delivery and looks for HIV itself in a blood sample collected from the baby. If the test is negative, it would be repeated within a few months after the birth to look for HIV again."

"If it's that low a percentage; how is HIV transmitted then?" I asked.

"Researchers are not exactly sure when babies are infected with HIV during pregnancy. It has been said that a small percentage of all babies are infected with HIV while developing inside their mothers' uteruses. However, this has not really been proven. It is known that the vast majority of infections occur during labor or after the baby is born and also if breast-fed by his or her mother.

"Throughout pregnancy, a developing fetus has his or her own blood supply. In other words, the developing fetus does not come into contact with the blood of his or her mother. This helps protect the fetus from infections in the mother's blood, such as HIV. However, developing fetuses do receive nutrients and various proteins, such as immune system anti-bodies, from their mothers. While a mother's HIV may not enter the fetus, her antibodies to the virus will. These antibodies cannot harm the fetus, but will cause the baby to test positive to an HIV antibodies test when he or she is born.

"At the time of birth, a baby often comes in contact with his or her mother's blood. If the mother's blood enters the baby's body, this is when HIV can be transmitted."

My head was starting to spin with all this medical talk but it was something that was definitely needed. I'd learned a long time ago that it's better to sound stupid asking a question rather than being stupid by not knowing at all.

"How can we or should I say, what can we do to reduce the risk of transmission?"

Dr. Norton took a sip from his coffee mug, then answered, "First, it all starts with the proper drug therapy."

Lia cut him off, "Which would you recommend?"

"There is only one that is approved by the FDA. It is called Retrovir. It's a three-part program. I'll write you a prescription for it now.

"The way it works is you'll take it for the next six months, prior to giving birth. I want you to take it twice a day. Once you deliver, whether it is by vaginal birth or C-section, you'll have to take a higher dosage of Retrovir through an IV. Finally, we'll give the baby a liquid form of Retrovir immediately after birth and continue it for an additional six weeks."

"So there are regimens but this is the only one approved by the FDA?" I asked.

"Correct."

"You said the proper drug therapy is the first step in reducing the baby's chance of contracting HIV; what are the other two?"

"This is where it becomes a little complicated. The second would be the type of delivery. Though there is no study that shows vaginal birth puts the baby at greater risk of being infected, it is believed by most that a C-section will greatly reduce a woman's risk of passing along the virus to her baby at the time of birth."

I was totally lost. "I'm sorry, doctor, I'm slightly confused."

"The thing is that some doctors believe that since a C-section is a type of surgery, there are risks of infection and other complications. Some believe that a combination of anti-HIV drugs might do a better job of stopping transmission, without even needing a C-section. According to some studies, an HIV-positive pregnant woman who has an undetectable viral load at the time of birth, the risk of delivering a baby infected with the virus is less than two percent."

"So it sounds like to me you don't recommend having a C-section?" I guessed.

"No, actually I would recommend having one. Even though no study confirms having a C-section and taking recommended drug therapy will greatly reduce the chance of transmitting the disease further, my personal belief is that it does. What I like to do is what is called a bloodless C-section. In a normal C-section, a needle is inserted into the woman's spine and injected with morphine. This causes numbness from the waist down, allowing me to make a long incision under the bellybutton to remove the baby.

"With bloodless C-section, the blood vessels near the womb are welded, or cauterized, using a laser to prevent them from bleeding. This procedure lowers the risk that the baby will come into contact with your wife's blood."

"Wow! You are really giving us a lot to think about. I'm afraid to even ask what the last step is but you might as well continue," Lia shot at him.

Dr. Norton cracked a smile. "The last thing isn't as complicated, Ms. Reid. Lastly, you'd need to formula feed in place of breast-feeding. Breast milk can carry HIV too, and breast-feeding adds considerable risk of transmission. As with transmission via blood, there are some indications that risk increases along with viral load. So far, research shows that the risk of breast milk transmission is highest in the first six months of life. However, there is no threshold or time point beyond which it becomes absolutely safe to breast-feed."

I was having another dumbfounded moment. "What is viral load? I've heard you use that term a lot and thought I'd just ask."

"Mr. Reid, how many times do I have to tell you to ask as many questions as possible until you feel comfortable about the situation? Viral load is the amount of HIV in the mother's blood."

"Okay," I replied.

Lia looked at her watch and realized she was really pressed for time.

"Is there anything else, Dr. Norton?" she asked.

"If you don't have any more questions for me, then that is about it. I'll see you back here in four weeks. I also want you to schedule an appointment for next week with our nutritionist. She'll be able to help you satisfy your cravings and will also set up a good diet to make sure you eat right.

"Ms. Reid, we've talked a lot about the baby and how to reduce the risk of transmitting the disease to him or her but please don't lose sight of your own health. I don't mean just while you are pregnant. Taking good care of yourself while you're pregnant is important. It's just as important that you pay attention to yourself after your baby is born. I see it all the time. Lots of women have trouble keeping to their pill schedule once the whirlwind of nursing and feeding and cleaning begins. It's fine to stop all your drugs. What I'd suggest though is switching to a simpler regimen. We'll have time to discuss this further in more detail when it gets closer to the birth.

"I'm also writing you a prescription for a drug called Epivir. You'll take it once a day. Please make sure you don't mix up the dosage and take the wrong one twice and the other one once. I'm writing this down for you. Take both in the morning when you wake up and Retrovir again after dinner or before you go to bed."

Lia stood up in anticipation of leaving.

"Baby, go ahead and get out of there so you aren't late. I'll just drop off your prescription for you after I leave here. I'm not going to go back to work."

Lia agreed and headed for the door. It wasn't long before I soon followed.

Chapter 17

The trip to Dr. Norton's office was very educational. I never truly understood just how complicated trying to have a baby while being HIV positive could be. Thankfully, it was an experience I'd live vicariously through my wife. I was afforded the luxury of being able to take my regular HIV medication. I only had one pill a day to take while Lia had to take that as well as an additional two more to reduce the risk of transmitting the disease to our child. I was definitely happy to be a man.

You always hear women complain about how they wish roles were reversed and men were the ones having children so we could experience the pain. I have a hard enough time trying to get a turd out of my ass when I'm constipated and you want me to push a six-pound baby out of my ass? Can you say HELL to the NO?

Some people can deal with pain like it's nothing. I, unfortunately, wasn't one of them. Pain definitely wasn't my specialty. If you were to look up the word "pain" in the dictionary, you'd definitely not see a picture of me. And after hearing how much my mother complained about my birth, I knew this wasn't one of those situations that was as bad as it sounded.

Shoot, the way my mother made things seem, I wasn't even sure if I wanted to be in the delivery room when Lia was having our baby. I probably would have been a lot safer it I kept my black ass out in the waiting area until all the hard work was done and the dust had cleared. I'd seen too many movies where husbands were getting cussed the hell out in delivery rooms. I wasn't looking forward to being Lia's doormat during those intense moments.

Especially not after hearing horror stories about women being in labor for fifteen to twenty hours. Lia might mess around and say the wrong thing. Instead of starting a new chapter in our lives, we'd be closing the door to our marriage. Lia never had a problem finding the right words to describe how she was feeling without having a baby exit her body. Think of what she'd say if she did.

***

The plan was to work from home that night but instead I daydreamed about how our lives would change once they baby came. Though I was extremely excited about being a father, I was also stressed. Being a parent was true pressure but it was on, I knew what I was up for. In a sense, I think I needed my child more than my child needed me.

Because of my unborn child, I never lost my will to live. I think if I had, neither Lia nor I would have made it as far as we did. The thought of that made me wonder about how many other people lost their will to live because they found out they were HIV positive.

I can remember when I first found out I was positive, I asked just about everyone I knew what they'd do if they found out they were positive. After a while, folks started to question my reasons for asking before offering advice. I'd play it off whenever they did and made it seem like I had a friend who was afflicted to ensure I'd get an answer without further questions.

Unfortunately, the words of comfort and encouragement I was searching for were never found. Instead I found out how little people really knew about the disease outside of the long-term effects it could possibly have on your body and that it was deadly. If I ever wanted to really find anything out, I would have to do my own research. Once I did, I saw a lot of alarming statistics that gave you hope on your life and the type of future you could lead.

The ringing of the telephone broke me from my thoughts.

"Hello," I said into the receiver.

"Can you talk?" Kenny asked.

"Sure, I was just sitting here attempting to get some work done. What's going on?"

"I'm still being pressured by them boys. They are really after you for that murder beef. I'm going to ask you again, is there something I should know about?"

"Nigga, I've already told you that I don't know shit about it. What were they asking you this time?"

"That is the thing. They weren't saying much of nothing. They just keep coming around watching me like I'm Osama Bin Laden or some shit."

"That doesn't make sense."

"That is the same shit I was thinking so I decided to walk my black ass over to them earlier. I asked if I could help them with something."

"The fuck you do that for? Damn, and you wonder why cops don't like your ass. You have no damn common sense."

"Man, I've played this game enough to know the rules. They don't have anything on me. What do you think, I'm stupid or something. If they didn't want me to know they were there, they would have done a better job hiding themselves. It was obvious they had something they wanted to get off their chest or a message to relay."

"But still, antagonizing the police is never a good idea. It's one thing if they are fucking with you, but you going to the car was like a slap in the face or something."

"Fuck them fools. They keep fucking with me. They just sit there, stare, and smile at me all damn day long. That shit is bad for fucking business. They know that. That is their fucking purpose."

"Is that what they said?"

"Naw, they asked if I'd seen you around and I told them not in a couple of days. Then the bastard goes on and says that he heard you were having a baby. How the fuck do they be finding shit like that out?"

"You'd be surprised! So what else they say?"

"Nothing much really or should I say nothing I wanted to hear. I kept saying neither you nor me had anything to do with that beef so they needed to find the right tree to piss on and leave me the fuck alone."

As Kenny was talking, I heard a knock at the door. I walked to the door and looked out the peephole. Speak of the fucking devil.

"Marco, are you still there?"

"Yeah, I'm here but you'll never guess who is at my damn door now."

"Got Damn! These boys are plucking my last fucking nerve. I swear."

"Kenny, I'll hit you back and fill in the blanks later. I'm about to entertain these cock suckers."

"That's what's up," he replied prior to hanging up the phone.

I answered the door. The expression on my face didn't hide my displeasure.

"Good evening, gentlemen. Is there anything I can do for you?" I asked sarcastically.

"Sure, you can confess and turn yourself in."

"I'd love to but then the city would have another innocent man in jail while a killer is running around on the streets, free to commit more crimes against humanity. I don't think that will fit in your slogan of *To Protect and Serve*."

"Very funny, Mr. Reid, but I'm sure the killer we are looking for is right in front of us."

"That is very interesting, Detective. Do you have any evidence to support this theory or is this another attempt at harassment? I'm sure you know exactly what harassment is, you know what you keep doing with my brother? That!"

Detective Benson laughed. "Did Little Kenny call Big Brother and tell him the police were harassing him? I thought he had a little more balls than that. I damn sure didn't expect him to bitch up like that. Anyway, it was just a coincidence we happened to be in the same neighborhood as him.

"Speaking of coincidences and neighborhoods, a witness puts you in Mr. Jenkins' neighborhood a couple of hours before he died. I found that quite interesting. Also, the same witness has your brother, Little Kenny, in the car with you. Isn't that interesting? Do you have anything you'd like to get off your chest?"

I was no longer in the mood for witty humor. I was not only his prime suspect but he was now actually building a case against me. The only thing he didn't have was a witness saying I pulled the trigger or a murder weapon with my fingerprints on it, both things they'd never have. However, I've read about cases being made with less in the newspaper.

"Actually, I do have something to get off my chest. If someone puts me in the neighborhood a couple of hours *before* Mr. Jenkins was found dead, so be it. One, you never asked me if I was in the neighborhood that day or did I ever say I wasn't. You only accused me of killing him.

"I'll say this again, I didn't kill him. I have an alibi. You don't have anyone putting me at the scene at the time of the crime, so until you do, which will be never, I'd appreciate it if you stay away from me and my family. Now if that will be a problem, please let me know now so I can make sure Jackson gets on the phone with the commissioner. I'm sure he'd like to know about the unethical behavior of two of his best detectives. I'm sure he wouldn't appreciate knowing a detective was about to cost the city a million dollar lawsuit for harassment. What do you think?"

Detective Benson didn't lose his cool. He cracked that same infamous smile. "He might not but I'm sure he'd love for us to close this case and put your black ass behind bars. You play your hand how you see fit and I'll play mine the same way. Either way, at the end of the game I guarantee your ass will be pressing license plates or cleaning highways for the rest of your life. Have a good day, Mr. Reid."

"And you do the same thing, Detective. Oh by the way, in case you decide to have another one of these talks, make sure you contact my lawyer first. Do you need his number?" I replied casually.

Detective Benson turned and walked toward the car, ignoring my statement. I stepped out of the house far enough to see the dark blue Ford Crown Victoria parked in front of my house. Detective Lawson was sitting in the passenger seat.

I waved to him and it looked like he shot me the bird back.

You had to love them. The battle between them and me was like a heavyweight fight. I refused to lose though. I couldn't lose. This was my life we were talking about. I was going to be damned if I was going to live my life in prison for that bastard's murder.

Chapter 18

The time was reaching the witching hour and Lia was just walking in the house from her interview. She walked into the bedroom with lust in her eyes but pain in her heart. She needed to quench her thirst for pleasure one last time but also wanted to remove the pain she felt deep down inside. She no longer wanted to feel the pain that plagued her heart.

Lia quietly removed all her clothes. I was sound asleep in our bed. She'd been out all day and decided to take a shower to wash away the dirt. The hot water steamed up the bathroom and eased her tensed body. No matter how hard she scrubbed or how much soap she put on her wash rag to cleanse her body, it wasn't going to do the trick.

She exited the shower at least fresh in her much needed areas and headed straight for the bedroom. There was no need to dry off, no need to waste any more desirable time. Her body called for me and she listened to every word, loud and clear.

I was peacefully lying on my back with my right leg bent in the air. She'd almost changed her mind and decided not to bother me but her hunger had reached the level of starvation.

She reached in the top nightstand drawer and pulled out a bottle of kiwi-strawberry warming massage lotion that heated up with each touch. She squirted some over my chest and down my stomach. People often say timing is everything. This was definitely a clear indication of that. Just three minutes earlier I was lying on my stomach but switched positions because I was uncomfortable. This worked perfectly to her advantage and mine.

She began my neck, trying to awaken me and made her way down to the lotion covering my nipples. She gently brushed her tongue over each nipple, making them even more erect. The touch of her tongue on my body anywhere was the easiest way to turn me on. I was extremely sensitive to it and she knew it. I woke up quickly but still played as if I was still sleep. Trying to see how long I'd stay asleep while she was working her magic on my body seemed to arouse her more.

She continued to work her way down my body to my stomach. I flinched a bit. Anticipation caused my dick to rise the closer she'd become to it. With every inch, I'd grow a centimeter until it was standing straight up and as stiff as the Empire State Building.

She squirted more of the lotion into her mouth and followed it by placing me inside. There was no way I could fake sleep any longer. I was wide awake and stroking the back of her head as she slowly wrapped her lips around my hard shaft. The sensation of her hot but wet mouth working up and down my shaft, was enough to make me explode with ecstasy.

As she continued to work me in and out of her mouth, she began to masturbate herself with one hand and me with the other. I hadn't a clue what had gotten into her and, at that point, didn't care. Once she fully aroused herself, she entered my entire dick into her mouth. Though I'd never been with another woman since I'd met my wife, I'd been with many prior to her. None of them could take all of my dick into their mouth.

To others, it clearly wasn't an easy task but she was able to accomplish the feat as if it was nothing. The feeling was one that is hard to describe. It felt as if the further into her mouth I went, the tighter the grip around my dick became, and the more pleasure it brought me. I'd often heard the accomplishments of the infamous Superhead. All the movie and rap stars talked about her as if her tongue was golden. On that night, Superhead couldn't touch my baby.

She continued to work me over with no intention of stopping until I came. She knew it took me longer to come from oral sex, than it would from making love to her. This didn't matter to her. She never stopped but rather became more increasingly into it. I loved every minute of it.

Every time she'd take my dick out of her mouth and lick down the shaft, a chill would creep up my spine. Every time she'd put it back in and fuck her jaws with it, I'd moan with ecstasy until I finally did what it was she'd been waiting for. Finally, I came and still she didn't stop. She continued to keep going until I was done and lying on the bed, quivering from the rush of making love to her mouth.

Once I regained my composure, I didn't want to be outdone. It wasn't that I didn't want her performance to outshine mine but I wanted to give her a pleasurable gift as well. Call it my way of saying thank you.

I rolled her over so she'd be lying flat on her stomach and poured the same lotion she'd used on me into the palms of my hands. I massaged her back, all the while planting sensual kisses strategically on her neck and the small of her back. As the lotion was absorbed into her skin, I blew a breath of fresh air from my mouth across it, activating the heating action.

Each time I'd do it, she'd squirm in excitement. I continued to massage her back for an additional ten minutes, then moved on to more pressing areas. I left her lying in the same position and started to lick from the base of her neck all the way down her back to her ass. Something really came over me because once I'd gotten there, I didn't stop. I continued to work my tongue down. I licked down the crack of her ass to the warmth between her legs. I wasn't big on tossing anyone's salad, not even my wife. It was a total shock to Lia when I continued to go down. Since she hadn't stopped me, it must have been a pleasurable surprise.

By the time I reached her pussy, it was already dripping wet and waiting to be touched with the same passion. I made sure not to disappoint it either. I worked my tongue inside her from the back while gripping her butt cheeks firmly with both hands. She began to roll her eyes and moan.

She firmly grabbed hold of the pillows and started to bite into them. I knew I had her then. I stuck my tongue deeper inside of her and tasted all her natural juices. I was in a zone. I could barely breathe with my tongue knee deep into her from the back and her ass smacking up against my face.

I pulled my tongue out and went back up to her ass. I wanted another taste. I wanted to turn the heat up a notch more. I licked the crack of her ass again but this time worked my tongue into her hole. It wasn't the same desirable taste I enjoyed while eating her pussy, but it wasn't as nasty as I thought it would be.

Lia wasn't prepared for this at all. The minute I worked my tongue into her ass, she came. Her legs started to quiver while her body was shaking uncontrollably. I couldn't make out a word she was saying but her actions spoke loud and clear. Her movement began to slow down letting me know her orgasm was over. I surely wasn't.

I rolled her over on to her back and decided why not allow her to taste her own ass. Some women probably would run from trying to kiss their man after he just ate them but not my wife. As I worked my way up from her belly button to her neck, she stuck her tongue out anticipating me kissing her.

Our tongues intensely wrestled with one another. Our kiss was deep and passionate, all the while fulfilling too. My once tired dick began to rise again, awaiting more action. Lia must have felt it brushing up against her inner thigh. She began to stroke it with her hand, bringing it to a fully erect status.

"I want you inside me," she softly said in my ear after she nibbled on it.

The way I was feeling that was just fine with me. I wanted to finally get inside her as well. With the hand she already had in place, she guided my hardness inside her. Extremely wet from all the earlier excitement, it eased in with no problems. I slowly worked myself in and out of her.

We began to passionately kiss again. My paces gradually picked back up. I reminded myself to slow it down because I wanted to enjoy every minute of it. I didn't want to rush anything and come again. She wasn't making it any easier on me either because she was now into it. She began to pull me into her deeper and faster.

"I want to get on top, baby!" she said.

I knew why. She could be in total control if she was on top. I didn't mind. Actually whenever I came while she was on top, it was always harder and more intense. I granted her her wish and rolled over onto my back. I allowed her to ride me except it wasn't my dick I let her ride. I positioned her on my face instead. I wanted another taste of her sweet pussy.

I carefully positioned her clit right over my mouth and began to suck on it while moving her hips back and forth. Our bed was set up right in front of the window. She grabbed a hold of the window pane. I opened my eyes, looked up, and noticed how beautiful she was in the midnight light.

She was lost within our passion. She grabbed a hold of my head and continued to stroke her body on my tongue. I got an uncontrollable excitement from what she was doing. I actually think I got more pleasure from eating her than I did fucking her. Her pace was now out of control as she came repeatedly. The feeling of my tongue pulsating on her clit became unbearable.

She jumped off my tongue quickly. She turned around and slid back down to my dick and put me back inside her. She knew this wasn't one of my favorite positions because I couldn't look deep in her eyes or see any of her facial expressions. I couldn't even occasionally sit up and suck on her titties. In this position, I couldn't do nothing but sit back and let her ride while I stared back. Sitting back wasn't my thing. Though most might allow their spouses or significant others to ride out while they are on top, I still wanted to put in a good stroke game. I made it seem like I was still on top throwing it back at her while she was riding out.

Since she'd exhausted a lot of energy coming while she rode my tongue, it took her a minute to get fully back into the groove of things. I wasn't mad though. I'd put in a lot of work eating her and honestly, was on the verge of coming that way. I needed that cool-out moment just as much as she did. Eating pussy was damn right erotic to me.

As she slowly paced herself on top of me, I sat up and licked up and down her back. I could see she loved the feeling of my tongue going up and down her body. I reached around, got a firm grip on her breast, and tried to position my dick further in her. This seemed to get her going.

I noticed her pace had picked up drastically. I leaned back to get deeper inside her and also to stop myself from coming during the process. I grabbed ahold of her hair and pulled her back. It was on. She continued to moan and scream in ecstasy.

"Yes baby! Fuck me, Marco! Fuck Me!" she cried in pleasure.

She had to keep quiet. Her talking while I was working was only going to make me come. I loved the sound of her voice letting me know how much I was pleasing her. People who don't think sex is purely mental are absolute fools. I could go on and on with the right mindset. But with us talking back and forth and me knowing exactly how much I was pleasing her always made me come instantly. It was as if I was coming because I knew I was pleasing her.

I glanced to the side to concentrate on something while she was coming to prevent me from doing the same. This feeling was out of this world. It was as if we had fucked, made love, and had sex all within the same night within the same session. I never wanted it to end.

Luckily, I didn't have long until she came again. Normally I would have allowed her to get her composure back while we switched to another position, but this time I was too into it. She didn't come as hard anyway so her mouth and motor continued to run.

"Come fuck your pussy!"

I rolled her over onto her back and decided it was time. It was time to put in my work. I knew the chances of us making it to another position within this session weren't good once I got on top. I was right. She wrapped her legs tightly around me. I worked my tongue in and out of her mouth while stroking her slowly. Her pussy was nice and adjusted by now to take me all the way in her stomach.

She loved when I'd punish her pussy and that's actually what I was going to do.

"Fuck this pussy, baby. Fuck your pussy!"

If I had any confusion to what time it was, that was the sign right there.

I propped her legs up and held them there by placing my arms underneath them and locking them into place. I put myself as far in her as I could get. She tried to move back a bit, but she was already locked into place and couldn't go anywhere. Part of me wanted to stop and try something else to keep it going but I was ready to come. I needed to come. My strokes were now pumps. I threw my body into hers and the audio from my pelvis area hitting up against hers was loud enough for the neighbors to hear.

"Fuck this pussy, baby. Ooh daddy, FUCK YOUR PUSSY!"

I pumped harder and harder while we started to uncontrollably kiss one another. I could feel myself about to come but it just wouldn't happen. It was as if my dick was paralyzed or numb. I loved it. The sensation of my sperm at the tip of my dick ready to ooze out but yet still holding still, that feeling was irreplaceable. She broke our kiss and started to bite into my neck.

"Baby, I love you. I love you so much. Fuck this pussy, Marco. Fuck your pussy, daddy!"

"Umm, I love you too baby. You are my baby!"

The minute I uttered my first word, that was what was needed to push me completely over the edge. I came so hard that I blacked out for a good thirty seconds. Within that span I couldn't see or hear anything. I had no clue what was going on. Once my senses started to come back to me, I tried to control my breathing again. As I started to pull out of her, I noticed the dried tears that lay on her cheek. I'd seen my baby cry many nights before but never because of how hard she had come or how good the sex had been. The sight of those tears was a feeling I'd never forget.

Chapter 19

The church was in dead silence. I was still in total shock. I didn't understand why the Lord would even allow Lia to have the notion to take her own life. What was I supposed to do? How was I supposed to continue living? She was the reason why I woke up every morning with a smile on my face.

How could I have not seen this coming? The signs had to be right in front of my face. How did I miss them? I replayed the events of the past couple of weeks and still couldn't see anything visible. She seemed so normal, so upbeat and pleasant about everything.

She'd finally decided what she wanted to do in life that would make her happy. She was looking forward to having our first child and the start of our family.

The baby! Tears began to form in my eyes. Not only did I lose my soul mate but I also lost my child. My baby didn't even have a chance to enjoy life at all. She never would be able to go on a date or to the mall. He'd never be able to drive a car or play football. I'd never get to lay eyes on what my wife and I had created through our love. Punishment? No, this wasn't punishment but rather torture in my eyes and a burden on my heart.

"What did I do?" I mumbled. "Why?" I shouted, not caring where I was or who heard. "What the fuck did I do? Why am I being punished? Why would you take my fucking family? What did I ever do to deserve this?" I yelled during the middle of the funeral.

Her funeral was closed casket, at her request. People came up to the front row to give her mother, father, and I hugs and their condolences.

Everything and everyone was at a standstill. Everyone stopped whatever it was they were doing and all eyes were on me. People were trying to give me time to collect myself. Unfortunately, they were sadly mistaken because that wasn't happening.

I looked up at the ceiling with tears filled in my eyes still screaming, "Why the fuck would you take my wife? Why? You call yourself a merciful God but no mercy was shed up my wife. Is it because I'm not praising you correctly? I mean, what am I doing wrong?

"Maybe I'm not putting enough in the collection plate during tides. Please, tell me what it is that I'm not doing so I can wake up from this horrible nightmare. I want to be with my wife again. There has to be something. I don't care what it is, I'll do it. Please, tell me.

"I need to have her beside me so I can rub her stomach or kiss her forehead while we lay down together in our bed. I want to be able to see her stomach go up and down as our baby reminds us of its presence with powerful kicks to her abdomen. Just tell me whatever it is I have to do and it's done. I'll do anythhhhh... I'll do anything. I just want my best friend back. Please, give my family back to me."

No one knew whether to comfort me or combat me for some of the vicious things I'd said. I was totally out of control and, to most, it was understandable. I didn't even hear my mother talking to me. Her comforting words were going in one ear and straight out the other. Usually she could be counted on as a calming spirit for either me or my brother, but I was facing the reality of losing my rock. Nothing would calm me down.

"Marco!" Kenny yelled. Though I tried to block him out, I heard him loudly and clearly. Since ignoring him was out of the question, I did the next thing that came to mind. I took my frustration out on him. He didn't have any of the answers I needed nor could he deliver upon my request.

"What, Kenny? What? What are you going to tell me? *'Everything will be alright.'* Bullshit! It won't be. You can't answer why He is punishing me nor tell me what it is that I did. Just leave me the fuck alone."

I looked up to the ceiling and continued, "What did I do? Why aren't you answering me? I just want my baby back. Please just tell me what I have to do to get my baby back."

"Come on, Marco, let's go for a walk," Kenny said as my mother continued to rub my back, trying to calm me.

I didn't move. I continued to stare at Lia's coffin, waiting for her to open it and get out. For all I was concerned, either she was coming to life or my questions would be answered on how to bring her back to life. Until one or the other happened, I wasn't going anywhere. My eyes were bloodshot from all the crying I'd been doing.

"Marco, come walk with an old lady," Mrs. Robinson requested.

For some reason, the sound of her voice calmed me a bit.

"Why, Mrs. Robinson? Why did He take my baby? Why did He take my family?"

"Come on, sweetie, walk with me outside so we can talk about it," she suggested.

I gathered what strength I had left and walked with Mrs. Robinson up the aisle to the main lobby. I still to this day don't know what made me get up from my pew or how I even heard or understood a word she was saying. Everyone else pretty much fell upon deaf ears or became victims of my wrath. The only thing that came to mind was that I had lost my wife but Mr. and Mrs. Robinson had lost their daughter. She knew exactly what I was going through. She could relate to the pain I was feeling inside.

She looked me in my eyes and said, "Marco, I need you to be strong, dear. Kalia doesn't know who this person is I'm seeing today. She would be very disappointed in how you are acting. This isn't the way she'd want you to honor her life by blaming Christ for her death.

"I don't know who this person in front of me is. I know you are hurt. We all are but I'm going to need both you and Phil to help me get through this. In order for you to do that, you have to be strong during these trying times. My daughter always called you her backbone. Right now, I don't see the strength that guided her through her tough times. Show me that strength, Marco. Show me that same strength that helped my daughter and shaped the man she fell in love with and I've come to love and look at as my own child."

"Mrs. Robinson, Lia was my strength. Everything I ever did in my life was for her or us. I no longer have that anymore."

"Baby, I know you want a person to point the blame on so why don't you point it at the true being responsible for this, Satan. He is the one who caught my daughter during a vulnerable state. He caught her at a time when she was deciding who to turn to for help and he convinced her no one could help her; killing herself was the only option. Blame Satan for his hate, not Christ for his love.

"She is home with Him now, watching over all of us. She is free of that hate. She is with her Father and savior. Though she is no longer here with us in the flesh, she will always be with us in spirit. Close your eyes and just free your mind and I'm sure she'll enter it and talk to you just like she was standing next to you now. The warmth that fills your heart, that is her love. She hasn't gone anywhere, Marco. She will always be with you. Nothing can replace the love the two of you shared, not even death. Trust me, she'll talk to you and show you she is still by your side whenever you need her."

She was absolutely right. I couldn't allow myself to fall into the same trap that Lia had. I needed to find out what my purpose in life would be now.

"Come on, the funeral is starting. Let's go back inside and take our seats."

"You go ahead, Mrs. Robinson. I think I need a minute to myself. I'll be in," I replied.

"Mom or Ma will do just fine."

"Huh?" I asked, a little confused by her statement.

"As long as I've known you, you've always called me Mrs. Robinson. You are the father of my daughter's child and her husband. I've always looked at you as my own child. You do not have to keep calling me Mrs. Robinson, trying to be respectful. Ma or mom will do just fine for me."

She paused. "I know you call your own mother mommy so I'd never ask you to call me the same," she said with a smile planted on her face.

In that split second, she was successful at doing what I feared would never be done again. She was able to get me to smile.

I kissed her on the cheek.

"Thank you, Ma."

"No problem, sweetie. No problem at all. Just make sure you aren't out here too long because I don't know how long I'll be able to last during this service before I break down too."

"I won't. I promise," I replied.

She turned around and headed back into the main sanctuary. I closed my eyes and tried to tell myself everything was going to be alright. I would somehow, through my family and with Lia's help, make it through the rest of this service without breaking down again. I walked over to the water fountain and took a sip. I wasn't thirsty but I needed something to wet my mouth. I put my head under the cold running water to calm my nerves, took a deep breath, and was ready to go.

"Hey, how are you doing, bro?" Kenny's voice said from behind me.

I turned around. "I'm doing better. It's still a long day ahead of us but for the most part I think I'll be okay. Mrs. Robinson really found a way to get me to see things the right way."

"You ready to go back inside?"

"I'm as ready as I think I'm going to get."

He put his arm around me. "You aren't by yourself. You hear me, man? We are ALL here for you."

"I know, Kenny. I know!"

Chapter 20

The funeral was very nice. Lia actually would have been extremely proud of the services. Outside of my earlier outburst, everyone else pretty much kept their feelings and emotions in check. Mrs. Robinson had a couple of times where you could see she wanted to lose it, but Mr. Robinson was right there to reel her back in.

As everyone headed back to their cars after the burial, I remained in my seat at the site. I always told Lia how I thought it was us against the world. It only seemed right that I said my final good-byes to her that way. The ground crew wasn't sure if it was okay for them to lower her casket into the ground. I assured them that everything was fine.

As I sat there watching her body being lowered into the ground, I could feel a part of me doing the same thing. I stood up and willed my way over to the edge of the six-foot-deep hole. Those four tiny steps were the hardest steps I'd taken in my life. All my hopes, my dreams, and burdens were standing on the hard soles of my shoes which felt like they were filled with cement.

I sighed. "Hey Lia! Thank you for helping me get through the rest of the day in a civilized manner. I almost lost it earlier and know you were the driving force behind that little speech from your mother. I'm not surprised though. It was something much needed and greatly appreciated. Even from beyond the grave, you know how to handle any situation.

"You've always been good at assessing a problem and coming up with the right solution. That is one of the things that I'm going to miss and also the very reason why I'm so hurt by what you did. I don't understand why you felt this was the best course of action to take. You didn't just take my wife and best friend away from me, baby, but my child also. You took away my ability to call myself a dad and a husband all in one swoop.

"I think I would have been a great father. I mean, we would have been great parents together. Why you would do this is something I will ever understand. I'm not even going to stand here and lie to you; I'm so pissed at you right now.

"You could have come to me. You could have talked to me. No problem was that bad that you had to resort to this. Now I'm faced with living my life without its centerpiece. I honestly don't think it can actually be done, baby.

"Why would you even put me in this position? Didn't our love mean enough to you? In the past, I was always your source of strength and comfort. What was so different about this time, our final time?

"You hear that, Lia? Final time! That is a phrase I shouldn't be using while we are so young. We should be growing old together. We should not be reaching the conclusion of our lives together now."

The tears were streaming down my face again as I vented all my frustrations. I knew she was listening too. I could feel her around me. My rants weren't falling upon deaf ears.

I continued, "I'll never stop loving you. Please, never stop loving me and don't ever leave my side."

I kissed the petals of the single rose I had in my hand, and then threw it into the grave. I watched it hit the top of her casket. I cleared my throat.

"I love you, baby. Always and forever!"

***

I decided not to go to the repast and headed straight home. I knew I was going to need my family and friends in order to get through the rough times but that moment wasn't one of them. I just wanted to be by myself and wouldn't have been good company to anyone.

I tried long and hard not to think about anything during the drive home. My attempts were unsuccessful. All I could think about was the last night we had shared together. I remembered the sight of her cold body lying still on the floor of our baby's room. Nothing seemed to make any sense anymore but when did any suicide make sense?

I could see myself waking up that night after rolling over and not feeling the warmth of Lia's body lying next to me. I gazed at the bathroom with sleep-filled eyes and noticed the door closed but a bright light beaming from the bottom of it. I thought Lia was inside the bathroom.

I didn't find it odd that there was a dead silence in the air nor that I didn't feel her move when she got out of the bed. I just re-positioned myself back on the bed, trying to get comfortable and went back to sleep. It wasn't until I had to use the bathroom hours later did the whole scene capture my full attention.

My wife still wasn't beside me and there wasn't a sound to be heard coming from the bathroom. Yet the same light was shining underneath the crack of the door. I got out of bed and knocked on the bathroom door.

"Lia, are you in there?"

I waited. There was silence. I opened the door. My wife wasn't inside. Something was definitely wrong. It felt as if a lump of coal had entered my throat. The dead silence that eluded me earlier was now visibly clear. I walked out of our room and headed downstairs. She wasn't there either. There were no signs she'd even been downstairs. The trail of clothes she'd left on the floor to our bedroom when she first came home was still intact along with her coat across the arm of the couch.

Just out of habit, I glanced outside to our driveway for good measure and surely her car was parked right behind mine. That's when it hit me. She couldn't have been in any other place but upstairs in our baby's room. I headed back up the steps and to the baby's room.

When I opened the door my heart finally stopped racing. She was lying peacefully on the floor.

"Baby, get up and come to bed," I said softly, but loud enough to wake her. She didn't move or reply.

"Baby, come on. You know I can't sleep without you next to me. I'll keep waking up all night and end up grouchy in the morning."

The sight of her naked body lying on the floor and the images of the lovemaking we had just shared started to turn me back on.

"I know how to wake you up," I said with a devilish grin.

I moved closer to her lifeless body and noticed the empty bottle of pills lying next to her on the floor. It wasn't until that very moment did I realize the severity of the situation. I rushed over to her body and tried to revive her. Each attempt was unsuccessful. I just sat there, with her lying in my arms. She was gone. I didn't cry. I didn't do anything.

After probably the most passionate night of sex with my wife, she decided to go in our child's room and take both their lives. No matter how hard I tried to not think about that night, I knew those images would continue to haunt me not only for that day but for the rest of my life.

✳✳✳

I pulled into my driveway knowing that rest, rest, and more rest was what I needed. The past couple of days had taken its toll. I hadn't been able to sleep since that dreadful night. Every time I closed my eyes, I'd have the same nightmare over and over again.

I'd see each and every facial expression on Lia's face as we made sweet love that night. Then I'd see her body lying on the floor. I'd wake up in a cold sweat. After a while, I found myself staying awake longer and longer, fearing the nightmares.

I'd told Kenny about the trouble I was having sleeping and he'd given me something to help me make it through the night and hopefully through the week. As I was getting out of the car, the mailman arrived.

I gave him a pleasant wave and he continued on his way down the street to the next mailbox that needed to be filled. I went to the box and retrieved the mail then headed for the house. I wasn't in the mood to look at any bills, disconnect notices or whatever junk mail I'd gotten.

Once I got in the house, I went into the kitchen and threw the mail down on the table. I felt bad for not going to my own wife's repast but how many "I'm sorry for you loss" speeches could one person take? It wouldn't have been long before I would've snapped on someone just for expressing their condolences. That would not have been right or fair to them so it was best I went home.

I poured myself a glass of water and took out the two pills Kenny had given me. I went into the living room and lay down on the couch. This had been my bed and would continue to be it until I could go and buy a new bed. I vowed never to sleep in the same bed that Lia and I had shared ever again. If I had the money, I would have bought a new house. I was thinking about getting an apartment and renting my house out. There were too many memories within these walls.

No sooner than my head hit the pillow I was out like a light. I didn't wake up until someone's car alarm went off outside hours later. I sat up and wiped away the drool that was on the edge of my mouth.

I wasn't sure if it was a side effect of the pills I'd taken earlier but I was thirsty as hell. I went into the kitchen and drank an entire glass of water without coming up for air, then poured another one. I took the second cup of water and sat down at the table.

I briefly laid my head down for a second. It wasn't long before I felt myself dozing off yet again so I sat back up and shook my head to clear the cobwebs. It didn't work. I was dead tired. I finished my water. That's when I saw a cut-off notice from the electric company on the table. That struck me as odd. I should have had at least three weeks before they came out and cut my power off. Still, I ripped open the letter to double-check. I was right. I had plenty of time to send in a payment before they'd come out.

I decided to check the rest of the mail to make sure I wasn't behind on anything else. I had all junk mail except one. It was a plain white envelope and the writing on it was very familiar. It was Lia's handwriting. I checked the postmark date and it was stamped the day after Lia's death. That was impossible. It didn't make sense. Why would Lia send me something in the mail instead of just telling me? How could she the day after she died? I opened the letter and began to read to clear any and all confusion.

Marco,

First let me apologize for my future actions. I know I'd be going out of my mind if I lost you and I'm sorry I'm making you go through a pain I myself couldn't handle. Though my actions might seem selfish, I hope after reading this you'll at least be able to understand why and somehow find a way to forgive me. I guess the best thing to do is start from the beginning of my day.

As you know, I went in for the interview for the school program I was telling you about and well you know how bad I wanted this. I could finally do something that I truly enjoyed and which would make me happy. Since I wanted it so bad, of course I didn't get it. According to the director, they didn't have enough money in the budget this semester to approve anyone. He said I could start next year if I was still interested.

Why next year instead of next semester? Because I'd be in my first year of the program and the classes I'd need to take would be during the fall semester. I was pissed when he told me that. I'm like, that doesn't make sense to have all the necessary courses for someone starting out only in the fall but what more could I do.

I guess I can't really be mad though because they told me the same thing during the initial interview. That is why I made it a point to not miss the deadline and get in this year. I never would have imagined the program's funding would keep me out though. Though I was very disappointed, I looked at the bright side. I was accepted into the program. This was just another setback but a minor one.

It felt good to know my best effort was actually good enough. It showed me that this is truly what I'm meant to do but it's going to be a lot of work achieving it. I had a good sense of accomplishment earlier. I left out of that office with my head held high knowing that I'd been accepted and the others who left before me or who were still waiting were being denied.

Baby I was so happy that I decided to go to one of our support group meetings. I thought it would be more motivation for me, plus you've been getting on me so much about how much I'd been procrastinating to go with you. I know you are probably wondering why I didn't call you to tell you I was going so you could go with me but I felt like it was something I needed to do by myself. I'm glad I went too. It really opened my eyes to what I was about to do to my child. It helped me see how much I'm really putting my unborn child at risk.

Do you know how many vaccines and pills our child would have to take if he was infected? I know the doctor said the risk of our child getting it isn't as large as most people would think but everyone in that damn room was infected prior to getting pregnant and had a child born with HIV. I'm talking about every last one of them. I know the doctor said the risk of our child being infected was less than two percent but that's two percent of the entire population.

I can't see the entire population. I didn't hear their stories. I heard thirteen people today and eight of them had kids and out of those eight with children they passed the virus along to ALL of them. It got me to thinking statistics are like words, they don't mean shit. While hearing real-life scenarios and cases were more like actions. Trust and believe, those actions spoke to me much louder than the words the doctor gave us.

What type of parent would I be to even bring my child into this world with any possibility of being infected? Do you know if I was to pass it to my child that is something I'd have to live with for the rest of my life? Not you, but me. I'd have to live with that shit every time I fed my child a bunch of pills or see how that disease would eat away at my child's will and body. I wasn't going to do that to my baby.

I didn't know what I was going to do, but I knew I had to do something. What took the cake and made everything so clear was after I met with our good old friend Detective Lawson. He was waiting for me in the parking lot as I was going to my car.

I guess he followed me earlier. I wasn't sure, but he had to. How else would he have known where I was? Shit, this was my first time coming to a meeting in a long time. Baby, he was talking about how much evidence they'd built against me and how much time I'd do in jail but he'd make sure I didn't do a day if I gave them you. No matter how much I told him I knew nothing about what he was talking about, he didn't want to hear it.

I told him over and over again that you didn't have anything to do with Rashaad's murder and neither did I but he already had his mind made up. I even questioned the fact that they wanted you but had so much evidence against me. That didn't make sense. I mean, why would they think you killed Rashaad if all the evidence pointed toward me?

That's when I was able to see how corrupt and blinded our justice system really was. He said that they had a motive and an eyewitness that put me in the area the night of the murder. I couldn't believe it, all of a sudden there is a witness. Come on! He said that he knew it wasn't me though. He believed I had something to do with it but didn't think I actually pulled the trigger and killed Rashaad. That was where you came in. I asked him where was all of his evidence to support his theory and he calmly let me know that I needed to cooperate with him or I'd find out about all of that the hard way.

Baby, I tried to reason with him by telling him that you had nothing to do with that boy's death. He just wasn't hearing it. You were already convicted in his mind. That is when he made it very clear, either I gave you up or they'd charge me. I'd be the one spending the rest of my life in jail. He gave me forty-eight hours to decide. There wasn't a choice to me. I chose neither.

Baby, I know you would have tried to find a way to beat any charge brought up against me, but what if this was the one time you couldn't come through? Shit, even if you did, how long would I have had to be behind bars before my case went to trial? Plus, if there was a trial, everything would be out in the open. Everyone would know our situation. They'd know we were both infected with HIV. They'd know that I cheated and how I got it.

A trial would surely ruin our lives and kill me whether I was convicted or not. It doesn't help that innocent people go to jail every day either. There was no telling how this thing would play out if it went to court. It was clear that the best thing to do was totally remove myself from the equation.

I know you probably don't agree with my decision but why would you? I want to talk to you so bad about everything but I know that you are going to give me that "Everything is going to be okay" speech, and everything is not going to be okay, Marco. This is something I must do. For once I want to be the one who does the best thing for our family.

I just hope you never stop loving me; but most importantly, living your life. You've always been the strong one. I know you'll get through this. It might be hard at first and I'm sure it will be a long road ahead of you, but you always see your way through anything and I'm sure that this time won't be any different.

I just want you to promise me one thing. I want you to promise me that you'll stop doing what everyone else wants you to do with your life and have faith in your abilities as a comedian. That is your true passion. Please, rediscover it. I have faith in you. Always know that I love you more than I love myself and even in death will continue to love you. I'll be counting the days until I can hold you again.

Love Always,

Your Wife Forever, Kalia Diamond Reid

I could see the stain her tears had left behind on each sheet of paper. I didn't know how to comment after reading that. One thing was for sure, everything finally made more sense. I thought knowing why would some-how ease my burden; instead, it made it worse. It only pointed out that everything was my fault. Lia killed herself because of my actions.

I knew she had nothing to do with that boy's murder. She'd be alive and well today if I was a man about the situation and told the police all that I really knew instead of trying to protect someone. The only person I should have been concerned about protecting was my wife and unborn child. That chance had come and gone and I'd never have the opportunity to do it the right way again.

Chapter 21

I caught up with Kenny on Market Street. Though I tried to stay out of my brother's affairs, I knew he was over here up to no good. The minute he saw me he ran off all the questions that were at the top of his head.

"Hey, what's the deal? This shit must be major for you to bring your ass down here this time of night. What, Lia put your ass out the house again? I knew that lovey-dovey shit y'all were talking wasn't going to last too much longer. You too wrapped up in work to give that woman the attention she needs. It was just a matter of time before you got back to the old routine again."

My lack of a smile or laughter let him know exactly how serious I was.

"I wish it was that simple. I'm not sure if you remember Lia's ex. We had beef with him a couple years back at that club downtown, Mystic."

"You talking about that cat that lives over on Sixth Street? Yeah, I remember that nigga. What about him?" Kenny replied.

"Well, Lia ran into him earlier and of course he tried this hand again and she tried to let him down easily but this nigga didn't know how to take no for an answer. He followed her into the parking garage when she parked her car and tried…"

Kenny cut me off, "Don't tell me this muthafucka raped my sister!"

"No, but that was the plan. Luckily for her, someone was coming back to their car after her and they ran him off."

Kenny pulled the nine-millimeter Beretta from the hip of his pants and cocked it back.

"Say no more, we'll handle this." He turned to his friend standing over on the corner. "Aye yo, y'all tool up. We got some work to put in."

I grabbed Kenny's arm. "Naw Kenny, WE will handle this," I replied pointing to him and me.

"Nigga, is you crazy? I'm not about to let you get into this gangsta shit. You've got too much to lose. Me and my youngins will take care of everything. You go take your ass home and take your wife out to dinner or something so the both of you have an airtight alibi that features a room full of witnesses. I've got you covered."

"Kenny, you must not be hearing me right. WE'VE GOT THIS, you and I. Plus I don't want all these folks in my business."

"That's what's up then. It's your life and you've got to live it how you see fit but I'm warning you, this ain't no shit you want to concern yourself with."

"I've heard your warnings, took them under advisement, and made my decision. Now what's the plan?"

"Well, go and move your car and park it in that handicap spot. I'm going to let them know I've got this dolo and get Black Pooh's truck and give him my keys."

"What do you mean park in a handicap spot? What the fuck for? I'm not handicapped and damn sure don't have a sticker that says I am. I'm not trying to get a damn ticket."

"Nigga, I got this. Just go and do what I said or you on your own. You can pull your own capers by yourself."

Though I had no idea what he was up to, I went ahead and did exactly what he said. I moved my car and parked it in the free handicap spot at the front of the apartment complex. I locked my doors and got into Black Pooh's black Ford Expedition with my brother. The truck had deep dark tint on the windows that didn't allow one to see inside. As I closed the door, Kenny threw a .380 handgun into my lap.

"How many pistols do you have?" I asked sarcastically.

"What the fuck were you going to use, a rock?" he snapped back.

I ignored his reply.

"What was that shit all about? Why we taking Pooh's truck and why were you stressing over me parking in a damn handicap spot?"

"Damn, do I have to spell everything out for you? The police come around here like clockwork fucking with us. The minute they see your ride in a handicap spot with no sticker they are going to ticket your shit. If your car is ticketed at Market Street that pretty much eliminates you from being anywhere near Sixth Street, doesn't it? I think so.

"As for Black, I have him taking my car out to Mo County to run a red light or something. They snap big pictures of your plates out there. That eliminates me and Pooh knows to stop at a spot out there where he'll be noticed and get something to ear, maybe rap to a waitress or something. That clears him, though we have his truck. They'll know we have something to do with it, but won't be able to put the pieces together without an eyewitness putting us there and that, they'll never get. When I say I have this shit, nigga, I got it."

Damn! I had to say, I was impressed. I would have just taken my car to his house and handled my business and thought nothing else about it. This nigga had a serious plan and it was obvious it involved not getting caught.

"What did you get a degree in, how to be a damn criminal or something?"

He smirked. "Naw, it's just that jail and I don't get along too well, if you know what I'm saying, so I try to avoid it at all costs."

The drive up to Sixth Street was quiet. I didn't want to talk about what was about to take place because that would just give Kenny more time and opportunity to try to talk me out of it. We pulled up in front of his house. There was no sign of Rashaad. I should have known he wouldn't be home. Nothing was ever simple when you were up to no good. Why should this time be any different? Kenny turned the truck around and parked it on the other side of the street from his house. We sat and waited.

"So what's the plan when he gets here?" I anxiously asked.

"I doubt he has anything in there, but at the same time I'm not trying to underestimate this nigga either. We'll let him get inside the house and get comfortable, then we'll go in through the back. It doesn't make sense to do it out here and wake up the whole damn neighborhood and having them writing down tag number or giving descriptions of us.

"Plus, I have something special planned for his ass and I'm going to need all the time possible. I want his ass to feel the same amount of pain he was trying to put my sis through. Rape isn't one of those types of things you can just forget about. That shit fucks with your mind for the rest of your life."

We sat outside Rashaad's house for a good two hours before we decided to make a dash for it and try another time. I told Kenny everything that had happened today so he thought Rashaad was just trying to lay low in case someone was looking for him. He figured he'd be home in a couple of days, so maybe it was best to come back in a week or two.

I didn't want to argue with him and tell him I knew he was over-exaggerating. I did not want to tell him that Rashaad would definitely be home tonight because he really had no reason to keep his guard up, That would blow my cover and then I would have to tell Kenny the truth. Once we got back to Market Street, I told my brother I'd keep him posted if I found out anything about RaShaad's whereabouts and he said he'd get back up with me next week to finish things off. After that, Kenny went back to join his friends and got high.

I never understood how they could smoke the same dope they were supposed to be selling. Any other time, I would have just stayed out there with them because I was guaranteed to be cheered up and ensured plenty of laughs. I didn't smoke, it's just that they always talked about some of the craziest things when they were high and it was no telling what you'd hear. I'm talking genuine hysterical stuff. You could do an entire comedy skit just on the types of things they'd say.

Once I got to my car, a parking ticket was surely awaiting me. The damn thing was for three hundred dollars. I was pissed. I get a three hundred-dollar ticket to give me an alibi for a murder that wasn't even committed. I pulled out of the parking lot and should have been heading for my house, but returning to Sixth Street was my destination instead.

It was something just burning in my gut telling me Rashaad would come back home that night and I wanted to be there when he did. It didn't help that I still had the .380 my brother had given me earlier. If my gut was right, I could always go to a pay phone and call Kenny and let him know Rashaad had come home after all.

Once I pulled up in front of his house, there was still no sign of him being home. All the lights were off in the house and his car was still missing. I started to question my actions and thought maybe I should have just taken my ass home to be with my wife. I decided to stay a bit but I wasn't going to say any longer than fifteen minutes or so. I parked on the same side of the street his house was on, but a house up so I could see him coming in my rearview mirror. There was only one way on his street and one way out.

The fifteen minutes I planned to wait turned into an hour and a half very fast. It was well after one in the morning and definitely time for me to go home. I turned my car on and started to pull off when I noticed headlights shining behind me from an oncoming car. I quickly put my car back in park, turned my headlights off, and took my foot off the brake so he wouldn't notice someone was in the car. I still left the car running because if it wasn't him, I was going to make a quick U-turn and get on my way home. That wouldn't be the case though;, the oncoming car pulled right into Rashaad's driveway.

"Jackpot!"

I thought about just going to the 7-Eleven down the street and calling Kenny like I planned to but decided against it. I wasn't letting Rashaad get away. It would be just my luck he was only coming home to change his clothes or something, head right back out and be gone by the time we got back. I had to handle this by myself and on my own.

I turned my car off and got out. I pulled the semi-automatic pistol from my waist and held it in my hand by my thigh as I crept up on his car. He still hadn't gotten all the way out of it. I raised the pistol up.

"What's up now, bitch?"

Rashaad looked at me with drunken eyes and reeked of alcohol. I wondered how he'd even made it home from whatever party he was coming from without getting a DUI.

"Look here, partner, you can have the car. Just let me get inside the house and then you can take the keys and go on about your business. It's not even that serious," he said, dismissing the fact that he was looking down the barrel of a gun. He even had a smile on his face like everything was a joke.

He started walking toward the house not even caring what consequences would follow. I remembered what Kenny had said about a ton of witnesses and why not to do it outside, so I followed closely behind him. I'd seen enough movies where someone was in a tight situation and they did whatever they could to get to their gun whether it was in the car with them or hidden under a pillow or whatever. I wasn't going to be the victim of this situation. Once he got the front door opened, I pushed him inside and closed the door behind me.

He immediately fell to the floor once I pushed him. He was having a hard enough time walking without me pushing him as it was. I turned on the lights so he could get a glimpse of me and see just how serious this situation really was.

"Do you recognize me now?" I asked.

He smirked. "Should I? I'm not really into men. Maybe I should have been though."

"I'm Kalia's husband, mutha fucka!"

He laughed uncontrollably.

"Is that supposed to mean anything to me? Hold on, hold on, maybe you'd like for me to be scared instead?" He started to curl his lips, acting as if they were trembling. He continued, "Nigga, I have fucking full-blown AIDS. Pull the trigger if that is what you came here to do. I could care less. You'd actually be doing me a favor, dawg." The look in his eyes was as serous as a heart attack.

It wasn't until that very moment did I realize that the man I was looking at was already dead. I lowered my gun.

"Stay the fuck away from my wife or the next time I come back we won't have the same outcome as tonight. You can bet your worthless-ass life on that shit."

He gave me that same smirk from before as he was trying to get up from the floor.

"Nigga, don't anyone want your bitch. I got all I wanted out of that pussy and left a little something behind special, just for the two of you. What you need to do is go home and tell that bitch to stop fucking ringing my damn phone before I give her something else to remember me by. I'm sure she'd like that. You should have seen how she rode me in the bathroom that day."

Whatever thoughts of compassion and leniency I was having were gone just as quickly as I raised the pistol back up. In the same split second I rang out six shots into this body with the last one in his head. It seemed as if every bullet that exited the gun and entered his body did in slow motion. He lay there motionless on the floor. It was finally over. I ran outside to my car and drove off.

Kenny was actually right. This was a road I wished I'd never traveled but now it was too late to go back. I never knew what effect it would have on our lives but knew I'd never be the same man again. I'd taken a man's life. No jail cell would ever compare to the jail cell I lived in my mind. I would be a resident of this prison for the rest of my life.

Chapter 22

I wanted to turn myself into the police and tell them I was the one they were looking for, but I knew that wouldn't bring Lia back. They closed the case before her body was cold anyway. It turned out there were no witnesses. The entire case rested solely on being able to flip Lia against me and it didn't work. At least not how they thought it would; instead of her telling on me it forced her to think she needed to take her own life to avoid going to jail.

I thought about filing civil charges against them but that would have only brought light to the pending charge against either of us and the reason for those charges. Also, I'd have to enter her letter into evidence and there was no way I was doing that. Even though I felt as if I no longer had anything to hide, I was still going to honor my wife's privacy.

One thing was evident though, I wanted to find a way to educate people on AIDS and HIV awareness and get them to see that there is such a thing as living with HIV. Lia made light about that in her letter of all the negativity she'd heard at her meeting. Maybe there are others who feel the same way she did and I could be of use to them. I could give them that positive reinforcement others kept away.

HIV and AIDS have always been cast as something purely negative. That was nowhere near true. The disease was no better than cancer or any other life-threatening one, however. people looked at HIV-positive patients a lot differently than cancer patients. It had people so afraid of dying that they forgot how to live. My challenge was surely ahead of me. How do you do this without putting your own personal business out there? How do you do it in a manner where everyone listens to you and what you are saying instead of questioning you and your motives?

Then it was clear how Lia felt about me pursuing comedy. It was her last request. How do I not honor that? But how do I honor her request and pursue comedy, and at the same time educate people on HIV and AIDS? The two didn't seem to go hand in hand.

It seemed evident that if I granted my wife's last wish and followed my dream I wouldn't be able to possibly save lives by educating people on being conscious of this disease: protecting themselves first, and being tested regularly; and if they contracted the virus, the importance of taking medicine and living your life. I was puzzled on which way to turn and needed something to take my mind off everything.

I decided to call my brother and see what he was up to. Knowing him as I do, he was out on the corner with the same knuckleheads smoking that stuff. The laughs from their conversation seemed just like what the doctor ordered. By the time I'd gotten there, the marijuana was lit and already in the air. I walked into a conversation that was in its prime.

"Man, have you ever realized how ass backward our society is?" Los said.

"Ah shit, here we go again. Why every time we get high you start this shit?" Kenny replied.

"What? I'm not starting anything. I'm just saying we are an ass-backward society. Why the other day I got an email talking about a gas boycott because of how high gas prices are? It asked everyone not to buy gas on Wednesday. Shit, I was down for the cause because gas is what, five dollars a gallon now? But I was on 'E,' so I went to the gas station Tuesday and got gas. That place was packed like it was a club on Friday nights."

Kenny cut him off, "What's your point, genius?"

"It made me think, if everyone was at the gas station on Tuesday who'd normally go on Wednesday, then what the fuck kind of boycott is that? The oil companies are still getting paid either way, just on Tuesday instead of Wednesday. Come on, if you normally make five million on Tuesday and five million on Wednesday but this week you make ten million on

Tuesday and nothing on Wednesday, you still broke even. That's ass backward and you know it!"

Black Pooh started laughing but Los had a point.

"Do you even know who starts those damn emails? The gas companies start them to make everyone get more gas the couple of days before. It's just like you'll hear rumors that gas is going to go up on Friday fifty cent, so everyone tries to get more gas on Thursday since that shit is about to hike up. Then Friday come and you see no increase or it only went up a penny or two. That's the gas companies putting that out there. It's a better way to advertise and market your product, that's all. You can't knock the hustle. Everyone has one nowadays."

"I never looked at it like that. I know my dumb ass be right at the gas station with pump in hand," I said.

"Man, if you really want to switch the game up, start walking or catching the bus or Metro. The bus is going to run regardless so that's gas already accounted for. Get on the bus for a week and don't use the gas in your car. They'll feel that decline. That shit will hurt their pockets. Think if two thousand people said fuck it, we boycotting and not getting gas this week. You figure the average person spends anywhere from twenty-five to forty dollars a week in gas. You do that by two-thousand people and they lost fifty- to eighty-thousand dollars. Shit, think if you had more than two-thousand people? That's a hit right there. They'd lower that shit down to a buck and a quarter you get enough people to do it," Pooh said.

"Shit, I remember when gas used to be ninety-nine cent back in like 1998-99. Take me back to them days," Kenny said.

"You sound like my mother and shit," Los shot back. He changed his voice trying to sound like an old lady. *"I remember when back in my day we used to swallow and not spit!"*

Everyone started laughing.

"Nigga, you still swallow, queer boy," Kenny replied.

"Shit, let's just be happy Los isn't bringing up that damn Bin Laden shit again. I swear he be killing me with that," Pooh said.

"Y'all just hating because y'all know I'm right. Bin Laden works for the

CIA. I don't care what no one says. I just find it funny how we know where he is, what he is doing, and when he is supposed to do something can't find him to save our lives. How we have all this so-called intelligence but the main piece of info we need, we don't have?

"Look at that whole Saddam situation. This man wasn't doing shit different for the past ten years but then all of a sudden during election time he was this serious threat. Get the fuck out of here. Here he is dead and gone and still we haven't found any weapons of mass destruction.

"Dawg, I'm up on Bush's game. He had them boys on the payroll. He don't fool me. Who in the hell can find someone hiding in a fox hole in the middle of the desert with camouflage bushes and shit over top it? Then this dude didn't even look like himself until a month after bathing once we caught him BUT they knew exactly who he was. You want to know how they knew, Saddam told Bush where he was hiding. Bush cashed that check too, 'cause right after that, them votes started to pour in. Even niggas was voting for him off that shit. Ass backward champ, we are ass backward!"

"Did you even vote?" Kenny questioned.

"Hell no! That nigga didn't vote," Pooh added.

"How y'all know what I did?" Los replied.

"True that, did you?" I asked.

"Nah, but still that isn't the point."

"But still my ass, you want to talk about how backward the world is but you not playing your part. You feel so strongly about this dude and you up on his game but yet didn't vote to make sure he didn't get in office. Haven't you ever heard the saying every vote counts?" Kenny said.

I decided to jump in and add my two cents. "Man, that shit don't really mean anything either until they do away with the Electoral College."

"That is so true. I mean, Gore had more votes than Bush in 2000 but Bush still got the nod because he had more electoral votes. What kind of shit is that? Why the fuck does Texas get thirty-two votes while D.C. gets three?" Pooh said.

"You know why and actually Texas gets thirty-four now. It went up in '01. They get it from '01 to 2010," I said.

"That's right and New York went from thirty-three down to thirty-one. A vote should be a damn vote. If you have more votes in one state than another fine, but just because your state is bigger than mine doesn't mean it should hold more weight. Shit, at the end of the day tally up all the votes and whoever has the most wins. Not whoever has the most electoral votes. That right there is ass backward. I'll give you that one, Los," Pooh said.

"My man!" Los exclaimed.

"But even with an ass-backward system, you still aren't playing your part, which doesn't make it better. Think how many other people feel the same way you do. If you have a million folks who think like you and don't vote and they happen to live in those *key* states, you'd see a bigger difference. But instead of voting, they talk about how their vote doesn't matter. That is the true problem right there. We are a nation of talkers." Kenny paused while taking another tote from the joint.

"Marco, remember what momma used to always say?" he continued. "You show me a leader and I'll show you people who will follow him but you'll never see a follower show you how to lead. That is America right there. We are a nation of followers who don't know how to lead.

"It starts with our president. How are you going to have a Commander in Chief who can't lead? He is following behind whatever Dick Cheney says. That is the real reason by the fucking war. Dick wanted to go to war and GW didn't have the balls to tell him no so guess what, he followed and now we've got kids over there dying and shit. Come on!"

"Hold on, champ, I'm not a damn follower," Los said in his defense.

"Then what are you?" Pooh asked.

"I'm a leader by far," Los replied.

"Oh really, then why are you out here every night hustling my product?" Pooh shot back at him.

"Your product, that's how we are going now? I don't see you ever going at Kenny like that. You are always going at me. This shit isn't yours anyway. It's the fucking white man's plan for the black community's destruction," Los retorted.

"It sure is and that proves my point also. You know that it's the white man's plan for our destruction but yet you still sell it which means you aren't doing anything but following everyone else who sells it and knows its true definition."

For once Los actually looked stuck. His reply didn't come back as rapid as it did before.

"Well, then you aren't any damn better because you know too and you still out here right next to me."

"Dawg, I said we are a nation of followers. That includes me too. The difference is, I'm not complaining about it. I'm content with my life and my status," Pooh replied.

"Why?" I asked.

"Why not? I don't have a degree like you. Shit isn't going to be readily available for me as it is for you. I accept who I am. I'm a criminal, nothing more and nothing less. It's as simple as that. Don't get me wrong, I'm not proud of what I do and there damn sure aren't any perks to this shit, but it's all I know and all I have."

"But that thinking is what keeps our young black men enslaved. I'm sitting here listening to everyone's views and points and that each one of you speaks with your own intelligence on what's going on in our society. But let them tell it and y'all are clueless and have no sense of direction. All of you do but aren't applying that sense. You don't have to stand out here trying to figure out ways to sell this shit and not get caught. All of you could really do something much more," I said.

"Marco, everything you are saying is right on point. I mean, you are really kicking some good shit but I like my life. I can't lie to you. You might think I could do better and you are absolutely right, but it wouldn't be what I want or like. I like being out here with my fellas, plus I actually serve a purpose.

"Now hear me out 'cause I know you are going to think this is the dumbest shit you've heard, but how many jobs would be lost without crime? You'd see a decrease everywhere, from police officers, to correctional officers at the jail, all the way to probation officers for when cons get out. We are talking about thousands of jobs, people just out of work. It's more stability in crime than folks think.

"It's not going anywhere, I'll tell you that much. Why, because the government doesn't want it to. I'm not a greedy nigga; that is why I'm still out here doing my thing. I stay under the radar and play my position. I keep a low profile. The only thing that matters to me is that all my niggas are eating and their families are good. As long as I can continue to do that, I'll still be out here long enough to retire."

"You think?" I asked.

Pooh started laughing. "No, but that's the plan. In reality some young nigga will come along wanting my real estate and he'll try to take it. We'll do battle over nothing and both of us will lose. Either we'll end up in a box or a cell over a murder beef, but I know that already. I'm cool with it. Remember, it's the life I chose and I'm living it, baby."

No matter how much I tried to reason with him, it was obviously too late to reach Pooh and the rest of them. I wondered how many other lost souls felt the same way Pooh felt. He was on point when he said we are a nation of followers. Shit, I chose a whole profession solely based upon another person. If it wasn't for my mother, I would have been a comedian.

Maybe I wouldn't have been successful with comedy and maybe I would have. Regardless, it would have been my fate set by my own terms and not someone else's. Why couldn't I do comedy and still educate? Just because no one else can pull it off doesn't mean that I couldn't. I didn't have to just talk about AIDS and HIV. I could speak on any social issues or topics that interested me. That is what most comedians did anyway. I could set my own platform, my own standard, and whether I succeeded or failed, I could still watch others follow my lead. I could step out of that mold of being a follower and now lead by example.

"You okay, Marco?" Kenny asked, breaking my train of thought.

"More than you know, bro. For once I'm going to take control of my own life."

"Huh? What are you talking about? I know you aren't talking about getting your own corner and start hustling, so what's your plan?"

"I'm about to make a difference by changing the standard and the expectation. I'll fill you in on all the specifics later. I've got to run."

"Look at what you've started now, Pooh. You've got Marco's head all fucked up and he wasn't even smoking," Los said as everyone started laughing.

"Naw, Pooh straight. Hear me when I tell you, I'm seeing things so crystal clear right now it's ridiculous. Let me break camp though, I've got some calls to make."

"You be safe out here," Pooh said while giving me dap.

"Naw champ, you be safe out here. I'm trying to see you get to that retirement plan you spoke so highly of," I replied.

Chapter 23

Tonight was the night I was going to take my career to the main stage. Once I made up my mind to return to comedy, I started hitting the local comedy spots begging for time. It wasn't long before someone gave me the shot I'd been begging for. The feeling after my first performance was unbelievable. I don't even think words can describe it.

I decided to keep my career change on the low for as long as I could but it wasn't long before my mother found out and I had to confess everything to her. The way she tells it, she called up to my old job and asked for me and was informed I no longer worked there. Of course that seemed awfully suspicious to her since I hadn't told her about having a new position with another firm, so the interrogation process shortly began.

She didn't hide her displeasure with my choice either but by the conviction and determination in my voice, she knew there was nothing she could do to persuade me otherwise. All she could do was respect my decision and accept it. If you asked me though, I think Kenny had something to do with her finding out everything. Had he had nothing to do with me getting my big performance that special night, I'd have been pissed but since he played a key role, I couldn't really say anything.

He was the first person I told about my decision because I knew he'd support me either way. He asked me if I knew what I was doing and if I was sure with my decision, and then he pretty much left it at that. When I had a show, he came along with the fellas from the neighborhood and I really impressed all of them with my routine. That's when he knew just how serious I was about comedy.

They say word of mouth is the best advertisement and they weren't lying. Los told his sister how good my act was and she came through with a couple of her girlfriends. She loved me. She loved me so much she decided to tell her husband because he was looking for an opening act.

It just so happened her husband was none other than Martin Lawrence. What were the odds? Martin had his people come down and check me out and the rest, as they say, was history. I still can't believe Los would waste his life away on a street corner when he had legit job connections through his sister. That was one mystery that will always escape me.

Once I was signed as Martin's opening act, I thought about telling my mother. I knew that once she could see that I could actually make a good living as a comedian it would be easier for her to accept, but the money wasn't nearly as good or steady as my old job so that wasn't a good idea just yet.

All day long I sat around waiting for the phone to ring to find out the show had been canceled or I wouldn't be needed to perform or something negative, but thankfully it never came. This just seemed too good to be true. Not only was I the opening act for Martin Lawrence, but the show was at the Verizon Center in my hometown, Washington, D.C. Talk about pressure. My first major show would be in front of my family and friends and most importantly my mother. I tried all day not to think about anything that pertained to the show and just relax.

Earlier in the day I got my hair cut, picked up my suit that I was wearing from the cleaners, and most importantly, took a nap. I left the house around 3 p.m. because I had to do a sound check. I wanted everything to be perfect. Walking through that tunnel at the arena and seeing all those empty seats that would be filled to capacity in a matter of hours was breathtaking. At that moment, I knew I had to rock it. This might have been Martin's show, but I was going to make sure everyone remembered my name before the night was over.

I sat in my dressing room and practiced my routine over and over until the clock hit 7 p.m. It was thirty minutes until show time and time for me to pop open a bottle of Remy as I did prior to my other shows. My nerves were always pumping full stream before a show so a couple of drinks was just the trick to relax me in the right state of mind.

This night, thankfully, Kenny was the only one who came backstage to wish me luck. I don't think I could have handled anyone else. Finally, the knock letting me know it was show time came. It was time to do my thing and that was exactly what I planned on doing.

✱✱✱

"Good evening, ladies and gentlemen. Nu Liphe Entertainment is pleased to bring you The Comedy Explosion Tour starring Martin Lawrence," the announcer said.

The audience began to cheer at the sound of Martin's name. I was jumping up and down backstage like I was getting ready for a heavyweight championship prize fight.

"Are y'all ready to get this thing started?" the announcer asked.

The crowd screamed, "YEAH!" in unison.

"Well, without further ado, put your hands together for D.C.'s own DeMarco Reid!"

The audience pleasantly clapped as I took the stage. My time was finally here.

"What's up, D.C.? How are y'all doing tonight?"

The crowd said, "fine" in unison quietly.

"Come on, y'all mutha fuckas can do better than that. D.C., I said how are y'all doing tonight?"

This time the audience's chant of "fine" was clear and distinct.

"That's more like it, got damn it! I know y'all can't wait to see Martin but y'all are going to know me up in this Mickey flick before the night is over. Everybody in here, except…any faggies out there. If you are gay the name I want y'all to remember is Martin Lawrence. Come on say it with me, M-A-R-T-I-N Lawrence. Don't forget he had on them little red shorts with the water *glisning all over his body.*"

I started laughing along with the audience at the line I used from his

"You So Crazy" routine. I used that time to take a sip from the drink I had made for myself to have during the show.

I continued, "Okay, before y'all get your man panties all in a bunch, I don't have a problem with gays. If you choose to like dick and you're a man, cool. You can like dick. That's your thing. Just remember, that's your thing and not mines so please keep a comfortable distance. I know y'all are looking at my ass so if you are going to look at it, please remember you are restricted to a five-second maximum look. Anything over five seconds and my ass starts to burn. If you can't follow instruction, I will have security escort your ass out of here on the spot...Shit, maybe I need to find a new choice of words."

The crowd started to laugh.

"*Come, on Mr. Security Man, ESCORT ME, Daddy!*" I said imitating a gay man's voice.

I continued, "My goodness there are some sexy-ass sistahs in here tonight. *HEY LADIES!*"

You could hear a handful of ladies reply, "Hey!"

"That's what I'm talking about. Ladies, trust and believe, before the night is over I'm fucking one of you tonight. Shit, depending on how drunk you are, I might even get two of you. Oh yes, the kid is getting some pussy tonight. Let me stop before I end up in court or some shit like Kobe did. *Yes, he put me over a chair and just rammed it in. I don't know what happened, officer. I was only checking to see if he needed some fresh towels and he took it.*

"Y'all ladies don't play. Y'all will take a brotha to court quick. I had this one chick take me to court just because I broke up with her. What the hell kind of shit is that? This chick took out a Peace Order talking about she was fearful for her and her daughter's life like I was a masked murderer or something, and I was the one who broke up with her. With all she did, you'd think it was the other way around. I'm like, what the hell, your honor, I don't want that bitch. Then I read the Peace Order and it all started to make sense.

"For y'all who don't know what a Peace Order is, a Peace Order is like a Restraining Order except you have to live with a person to get a Restraining Order in Maryland. We didn't live together so she had to get a Peace Order. Anyway, I'm reading the order and I noticed it said I couldn't come anywhere near her, her job, her house, or any of her relatives for six months. I'm thinking, thank you, Jesus, UNTIL… Until it dawns on me that I gave her ass a damn diamond tennis bracelet and I asked her for that shit back the night I broke up with her.

"That's okay. I only have two more months and then I'll be knocking on her front door to get my shit back. I ain't forgetting, got damn it.

"I can't stand y'all muthafuckas. I'm telling you. I see why brothas lose it. This chick didn't want to give me any of my shit back. I let this chick borrow a damn coat one night because it was cold outside and can't even get that shit back. Key word now is BORROW. She had the nerve to say I gave it to her instead of allowed her to borrow it. She even had the nerve to call me an Indian giver. What the hell? Didn't the Europeans say the Indians gave them their land, while they took the shit? You damn right I'm an Indian giver because I didn't give your ass shit."

I pointed to a light-skinned woman in the audience sitting up front. "I can't stand y'all asses. The minute I can buy a pussy on eBay I'm through with women. Think I'm playing? With my luck, the damn thing will come with a mouth and I'll have to take that shit back also. I'm sorry, women are just too crazy for me. All of you are just crazy.

"I remember once when I was a child, my brother and I used to talk back and forth to one another in Spanish. We thought it was a slick way to show off. Plus we could talk about girls behind their backs without them knowing. Well, one day we were out on the playground and this girl walked by. I think we were about ten or twelve years old.

"Well, my brother looked at me and was like *Hombre mira que grande es el culo de ella*. That means, man, look how big her butt is in Spanish. No one standing near us had a clue and I thought that was funny as hell. I'd be like *mira a estos pendejos tratando de adivinar lo que nosotros estamos diciendo* which means look at all these dumb asses trying to figure out what we are saying. We'd laugh our asses off as kids were trying to figure out what we were saying.

"We'd have to watch ourselves sometimes though, because every now and then you'd catch that one smart-ass girl who knew too damn much for her own good. She wouldn't know exactly what you'd said, just one word to fuck everything up. We'd be like *hombre mira que grande es el culo de ella*. The teacher would be like *Kenny, what did you say* and my brother would lie. Her smart ass would jump in, *that isn't what he said because culo means ass in Spanish*. We'd want to smack the shit out of her.

"Shit, once I said the same damn thing when a girl walked past, *hombre mira que grande es el culo de ella*. She turned around and was like *deja de verme el culo con tu sucia personalildad*. That shit fucked me and my brother up for real. Turned out the chick's mother was Puerto Rican."

I paused and looked at the dude in the front row. *"Mira a estos pendejos tratando de adivinar lo que nosotros estamos diciendo."*

Everyone started laughing. I looked back at the same light-skinned woman from earlier. "That joke went right over your head, didn't it, boo?" She couldn't help but laugh her ass off.

"I'm telling you, women are just crazy! Don't feel bad though. Even my mother is crazy. I used to wonder why my father was always in the basement when her ass was home. It's because my mother was crazy. When you are a kid, you don't understand shit like that. You couldn't tell my brother or me anything wrong about our mother back then. Now...I understand Momma didn't have it all upstairs.

"Who the hell gives their kid Robitussin for everything? If you let her tell it, Robitussin could cure cancer. I don't care if you had a cut on your foot, Momma was putting a Band-Aid on it and giving you a teaspoon of Robitussin. You could have the Ebola virus, she didn't care. *Baby, get the Robitussin out the icebox.*"

I stopped and looked at another woman in the crowd. "What are you laughing for? Shit hasn't changed, it's just different. What's the new thing y'all ladies use now?"

Everyone was quiet, waiting for me to answer my own joke.

"Don't be shy, come on and fess up to y'all shit. Amoxicillin. Better known as *The Pink Stuff*. You can't find a black house today in America, without a bottle of pink stuff in the refrigerator. It's right next to the grape jelly and barbecue sauce. The shit is so popular now, you don't even need a prescription to get it. I saw a bottle on sale in the dairy section at the grocery store for five dollars and ninety-nine cents."

People in the crowd started shaking their heads in agreement, while trying to catch their breath from laughing ecstatically. I turned and looked at a white woman in the audience and started scratching my head.

"You noticed how I said a black house. That's because y'all medicine of choice still hasn't changed. Your medicine of choice is a hospital. You'll take your kids to the hospital for a cough, with a slight fever. Nigga could have a temperature of ninety-nine-point-seven and y'all aren't taking any chances. *Bob, we need to take little Roger to the hospital.*

"Let that be a black family with a black child. His ass could have a temperature of one-oh-one and their little asses better put a cold wash rag on their head while they are getting ready for school. And we better not get a call from the nurse's office later in the day either. If I have to leave my good job to take your ass to the doctor, you better have something serious. I'm not talking any common cold or stomach virus. Hell no! You better be telling me my six-year-old child has an ulcer or something."

I started to laugh at myself.

I quickly turned serious. "But don't think you are off the hook, Becky. Y'all white women are crazy too. I mean, let's say you work as a hotel clerk at the front desk and I'm worth thirty, maybe even forty million. If I ask you to come to my room at two in the morning, why in the hell do you think I want play Uno? *Kobe, why are you pulling my undies down? What do you mean get on my knees?* I'm sorry, but that must be some Colorado-type shit because let you ask a woman in D.C. to come to your room at eleven a.m. *For what, nigga? I'm not fucking you. Oh no, you've got the game fucked up. We can meet at Starbucks or something. Nigga please, you ain't slick!* Women in D.C. know, come back to my room is code for we fucking."

The crowd erupted.

"Okay, that wasn't right. My bad, my bad. But y'all know y'all aren't right. What's the name of that group that sing that slutty shit? What's that song, 'Don't Cha' or something?"

"The Pussycat Dolls," a woman in the crowd yelled.

"What in the hell is wrong with them? They couldn't think of a better name for themselves. I guess not singing...*Don't you wish your girlfriend was hot like me. Don't you wish she was a freak like me? Don't ya?*

"Hell to the naw! If I'm wishing all that shit, how the fuck did she become my girl in the first damn place? She obviously needs to be replaced. But leave it up to a bunch of white women to come up with some slutty shit like that.

"The other day I heard my four year old goddaughter signing that damn song. I liked to slap the taste out of her mouth. It's bad enough she is going to grow up to be crazy like the rest of women do, but I'll be damned if she grows up to be a crazy *white* woman."

While half the crowd was grasping for air and the other half agreeing with me, I took another sip from my drink.

"What are you looking at?" I said to a hefty brotha sitting in the front row. "You mad because you can't drink on your job? Drunk-ass self! Don't be mad, Toine!" When he started to laugh, I noticed the many teeth missing from his mouth.

"Got damn! What the hell happened to your mouth? Ladies and gentlemen, please give it up for the former heavyweight champion of the world, Mr. Leon Spinks. Good Lawd, your mouth is foul. I know that isn't your lady sitting next to you with a mouth like that. You can tell you don't have a job with benefits. You probably have no idea what dental even is. I'm telling you. Do y'all see this shit? My man has every other tooth. What, do you have your teeth working eight-hour shifts or something?"

I was laughing hard as hell at myself.

"Let me stop, before you come up here and get your ass kicked. That's right, don't let the skinny part fool you. I have no problem beating that ASS! Let me leave you alone. You want a drink, partner? What you drinking?"

He ignored me, fearful of being the butt of another one of my jokes.

"No, I'm serious, my man, what are you drinking?" I asked again.

"Purple Passion," he replied.

I immediately started laughing.

"No wonder you weren't trying to tell me. What the hell is a Purple

Passion? Gay people even like *that's a punk-ass drink*. Somebody get my man a shot of Remy, quick!"

I headed toward the curtain leading backstage. "Can you make sure he gets a shot of Remy on me?" They gave me the thumbs-up, letting me know it would be taken care of. I headed back toward the stage.

"There you go, my man, a shot of Remy on me. Hold on, maybe I shouldn't say it like that. This nigga drinking Purple Passion and shit. Don't get no funny ideas. Fuck around and he'll be waiting for me after the show, talking about *Yoo Hoo, Mr. Funny man Come here so I can bend that ass over in eight-hour shifts*. Fuck that, remember what I said earlier, Martin Lawrence... red shorts *glisning* all over his body!"

The usher came down the aisle with the gentleman's drink I'd ordered.

"What the hell took you so long? You know I'm an opening act. I only have ten minutes to shine and you're wasting eight of them. Niggas always on CP time. Next time I order a drink, your ass better be here quicker; looking like Michael from *Good Times*." I paused and started to sing. "Temporary layoffs!" I was trying hard not to smile as if I was serious but couldn't help it. "Do you remember that part in the song? That is going to be your ass if you come late with another damn drink. Let me stop. Y'all give it up for Purple Passion and Michael from *Good Times*."

The audience applauded. I took another sip from my drink.

"Shit is good, ain't it?" I asked Purple Passion. He agreed.

"I know it is. Yours probably tastes even better since it's free, damn it. Anyone else want a drink?"

The light-skinned woman I was picking on earlier jumped up.

"Got damn! You just going to knock folks over with your titties, huh? All for a free drink. Isn't that a bitch? What do you want to drink, baby? For you, all I'm serving is sperm and you have to get it from the tap." I paused. "I'm just playing, sweetie. What are you drinking?"

"Rum and Coke," she replied loudly.

"Did you hear that, Purple Passion? She said rum and Coke. The lady is drinking rum and Coke and you are drinking a Purple Passion. Something isn't right with that picture. Can someone get the lady a rum and

Coke for me with a twist of sperm? I hope you don't think that drink is free either, baby; you coming back to my room. What does that mean again, y'all?"

"We fucking!" the audience yelled.

"That's right!"

While the audience broke out in laughter, I turned to Purple Passion.

"Look at Purple Passion. *What about me? I wanna go back to your room too!* You can forget that shit, buddy. Take your fluffery ass back down the yellow brick road with that shit Purple Passion. I don't get down like that."

I paused. "Nasty-ass muthafucka. These ladies out here are crazy but the fellas ain't any better. They are nasty as hell. I'm not talking about nasty meaning, they'll fuck-anything-type nasty either but just nasty-for-no-damn-reason-at-all nasty.

"Like a man will get in the shower and take a piss right there in the shower. Now just because he pissed in the shower isn't the nasty part, because he could have aimed right at the drain. But no, the nasty muthafucka is going to piss with his back in the water to the back of the tub, then push the shit forward to the drain with his foot. That is some nasty-ass shit!

"How many of y'all ever took a shit and when you went to wipe your butt you got a little shit on your hand? Okay, common error, no problem. The difference between a woman and a man is, a woman will know that she got a little bit on her hand so she'll wash it off. A man, his dumb ass has to check and make sure so he smells the spot where the shit is. Now this muthafucka got a shitty hand and nose and wash neither one. Just nasty, I'm telling you.

"Or how many of you nasty bastards ever took a shower after you cleaned your ass you noticed a little shit residue on your washcloth. Sounds nasty, right? Well, since most people don't know the correct way to wipe their butt I'm not surprised. The nasty part is this nigga just rinses the shit off and then washes his damn face with the same shitty washcloth. That little bit of soap didn't kill the damn shit. Nasty!"

While people were trying to catch their breaths, I took another sip from my cup.

"How many of y'all smoke weed?"

People in the audience started to reply.

"You can always tell when a person smoke weed by asking one question. Do you think they should legalize weed? Weed smokers will give you one hundred and one reasons why it should be legalized. Some of y'all don't need to smoke though. If you smoke weed so much, you put the shit on your grocery list, damn it, you have a problem. *I need to get some eggs, milk, a dime bag, some pork chops…* get the fuck out of here."

The same usher from a little while ago came back out to bring the light-skinned woman her complimentary drink.

"Temporary layoffs."

The audience erupted with laughter. I myself couldn't help but laugh at my own joke. Once everyone settled back down I continued, "I love y'all weed smokers though. Shit, I love chilling with my brother's friends when they get high, especially his friend Los. When Los is high, he is bound to say anything and it will be the dumbest shit you've ever heard. He'll fuck around and say shit you've seen on the Internet but you don't really pay it any attention to it because of how dumb it is. He'll be like…"

I started to pretend like I was smoking weed. "*Man, have you ever wondered how ass backward the world is? Like check this, we drive on parkways but park in driveways. What kind of shit is that? Or how about if 7-Eleven is open twenty-four hours a day, seven days a week, why in the hell do they have locks on their doors?*"

I stopped and acted like I was taking another pull from the weed cigarette.

"Y'all think this shit is funny but I'm dead-ass serious. How many of you watch baseball? You do, good. Have you heard of the Chicago White Sox? Well, if they are called the White Sox, why do they wear black socks? If you need more proof have you ever thought about this? Why do we sterilize the needle for lethal injection? Correct me if I'm wrong, but I think an infection is the last thing on that muthafucka's mind."

I started laughing, breaking my skit.

"Y'all got to give that shit up. Weed is killing your brain cells but how can you not laugh at shit like that? And what kills me is he'll be dead-ass serious too. The other day he was like, *the human race is doomed. I didn't even realize it until last night. I was sitting around smoking and started reading the labels of my household products...*

"Now right there, that should have been a newsflash that there was a problem. Who the fuck sits around and reads the labels on their household products but a nigga who is high? He was like, *I was eating a bag of Fritos and I noticed the bag said you could be a winner! No purchase is necessary.*

"Now we are all looking at him lost, trying to figure out what the hell he is talking about. We looking at each other like okay and then he explains. *Y'all don't get it? They are advertising shoplifting. If I don't purchase the bag of Fritos, then how else would I get them?*"

"For y'all that didn't hear me, leave the drugs alone because I will be forced to laugh at your ass. Once his ass was like, *do y'all use Dial soap? Why do they directions say use like regular soap?*

"Now I must admit that one had me. I ran straight to Safeway and bought a bar just to see if that shit was true and sure enough it was. How the fuck else are you supposed to use soap? Now my ass be sitting around like I'm high reading labels and shit. Talking about, why on the bottom of Tesco's Tiramisu dessert it says do not turn upside-down. Why would you put that shit on the bottom? If I'm reading it, it's obviously too late 'cause I have the shit upside-down."

I paused while taking another drink.

"The other day, I saw Los standing at the bus stop and the bus had just pulled off. He hadn't missed it, but for some reason didn't get on it either. I don't know why, but something kept telling me to ask him why he didn't get on that bus. It was obvious he was waiting for it or he wouldn't have been standing at the bus stop. I casually walked over to him and asked him and he asked me, 'Did you read the side of the bus? That shit said one out of twenty people on this bus are HIV positive. Now I have nothing against any of them but I haven't been tested yet and if I get on that damn bus that could meant I'm one of the twenty.'

"Any other time, I probably would have laughed my ass off. He was a perfect example of what the sign was saying. But instead of getting the message, he somehow convinced his self that by not getting on that bus, he wasn't going to be one of the twenty. The meaning of getting tested to know your status went straight over his head.

"How? Hell if I knew. This dude just doesn't have it all upstairs. When I went home, I happened to talk to my mother and decided to tell her. To my surprise, her response was *I don't blame him. I wouldn't have gotten on that bus either.* I couldn't believe my own ears. This was coming from the same woman who marched alongside Dr. King for a higher cause. Now she doesn't support HIV or AIDS awareness. Come on. I asked my mother, when the last time she'd been tested. This heifer goes and asks, 'For what? That is a young people's disease. I don't have to worry about that in my age bracket.' Like HIV or AIDS is just going to be like, oh no we can't infect her; she is too old. I need someone twenty-five through thirty instead.

"I'd say just crazy but women aren't the only ones thinking like that. I looked at the statistics and the one that jumped out at me is one-third of HIV-infected people don't even know they are infected. For those of you who don't know what one-third is, that is thirty-three percent. Here is how real this shit is. Tonight we've sold out this arena. That means that there are at least twenty-one thousand people here tonight. Let's say all of you have HIV, six thousand nine hundred and thirty of you haven't been tested and don't even know you are.

"That to me is scary as hell. We have to get tested, people. That is a must. People are so scared because HIV is always affiliated with AIDS. I am here to tell you that they are not the same thing. Also, whenever people hear the word HIV, they automatically think of death. I'm here to tell you that there is also a term as 'living with HIV.'

"Did you know that many experts say that if caught early, HIV patients with proper treatment can live out their normal life expectancy? Your life doesn't have to change, people, but if you don't know you are infected and don't get tested, not only will you affect your life but possibly the lives of others. Let's get tested, people. Let's make a difference. Oh and Momma, Robitussin will not cure HIV or AIDS!"

While people started clapping and laughing I asked, "What is my name?"

The audience replied, "DEMARCO REID!"

"I told y'all mutha fuckas you would remember my name before I left this bitch! That's all my time, D.C.!"

I threw the microphone down on the stage, then pointed up and pounded my heart twice. "Lia, this was for you. I love you, baby!"

Chapter 24

"It's hard to believe the ride is finally over. If you would have told me five years ago that this is how my life would end, I would have called you crazy. Shoot, if you told me five years ago this is how my life would turn out I would have said the same. Go figure, I can actually call myself a comedian.

"That is something I'm proud of but what I'm most proud of is the fact that I was a husband. I just wish I would have appreciated her more in the beginning. I'll never be able to get back all that wasted time.

"Please, don't waste your time, folks. If you take anything from my life, take the fact that wasted time is something no one can get back. It's lost forever. Spend every moment living your life to the fullest. You hear that phrase all the time. I know I did, but we rarely pay attention to it. I wasted a lot of time within my marriage. I'm thankful that Christ opened my eyes to what was most important to me while she was with us.

"I'm sorry I kept everything from all of you for so long but I had no choice. In the beginning, it was about not wanting your sympathy. Then it turned into us not wanting anyone to know our business. All of you are family and if you can't trust you family, then I guess you can't trust anyone. I honestly can see now that things would have been so different if we just would have confided in you or leaned on you for support.

"I wanted to respect my wife's wishes but I also should have asked her to respect mine. I could and should have handled this whole situation much better than I did. That is a part of growing up though huh, living and learning. Well, I can say I lived long enough to learn from my mistakes. Hopefully, by hearing my story you'll learn from them.

"Please know that today I'm not depressed or sad. I'm not confused or disoriented. I see things very clearly. This is truly my time. My life has reached the end of its course. It's time for me to be with my wife and child once again. The one thing I leave behind for all of you is my love and respect.

"Ma, thank you for raising two gifted children. I know it was hard when Pop passed but you did what most black women do when their backs are up against the wall. You rolled up your sleeves and got your hands dirty. I'll always appreciate you for that. Please don't view my passing as me giving up on life. This is just my time and I'm at peace with that.

"Mr. and Mrs. Robinson, thank you for never treating me any different than you would your own child. Most people would have just acted as if I was Lia's husband, but not you. The both of you loved me unconditionally as if I were your own. I apologize for not being able to stop Lia from taking her life. That is a burden that has always stayed with me.

"Los and Black Pooh, man, we had some good times. Hopefully I've talked enough about what y'all do for a living to make you have to give it up. Mr. Robinson, if I haven't, please make sure they change careers. The both of you have so much potential to do so much more with your lives. If you can get me to see that I don't need to follow everyone else's plan but rather be my own leader, I'm sure you can do the same for others. I'm not going to bombard you with suggestions because just as I had to find what made me tick, so do you. I only ask that you stop settling and find it.

"Kenny, I'm going to miss you the most. Besides Lia, you are the only one who truly knows me inside and out. I'm going to miss relying on you for strength and laughs. But I'll miss our talks more than anything. I know you'll probably question a lot of things about my death. You'll wonder why I'd do something like this but truly look within your own heart for the answers. They are right there. No matter what, always remember *Nunca olvides, todo no es como siempre se ve* or should I say *Nunca olvides, las cosas no son como suelen verse.*

"I love all of you very much and will miss each and every last one of you. Until we see each other again, I'll leave you with a quote from my favorite comedian Red Foxx also known as Fred G. Sanford.

"Elizabeth I'm coming to see you, honey. Lia, I'm on my way!"

Chapter 25
Searching for the Truth

Fresh air was calling my name. This was too much. I would have never expected any of this, before I came to Marco's funeral. He didn't leave a stone unturned. How could I have not known my own daughter was HIV positive? Why wouldn't she want to come to her mother or me no matter what we thought?

We've always been there for her. Something wasn't right. I've always trusted my first instinct and today wasn't going to be any different. There were just too many questions, not answered in that tape.

I waited patiently for Denise outside the church. She took her time coming out, trying to be there for Marco's mother just as she was for us when we lost our child. There were some things on my mind that I needed to clear up a bit.

"Neese, can I talk to you for a minute?" I asked my wife.

Right away, she knew something was wrong. It wasn't like me to be so rude but this was of an urgent nature. She excused herself for a moment, and then came to see what it was I needed.

"Baby, do you think you can get a ride to the repast with Kenny and I'll meet you there? I have to get out of here."

"What's wrong, honey?" she asked.

"It's nothing, I just need some fresh air," I replied, trying to downplay my suspicions.

"Are you sure, Phil?"

"I'll be fine, Neese. Do you think it will be a problem?"

"I'm sure it won't. I'll ride over with Margaret. She definitely doesn't need to be left alone at a time like this. I'm sure she won't object. Go ahead and handle whatever you have to. We'll talk later."

I kissed my wife and headed for my car. My next stop was the twenty-third precinct.

***

I walked inside, looking for Detective Benson or Lawson. I figured it made sense for this to be my first stop being as though my daughter was a suspect in a murder investigation that I had no knowledge of. Even if they didn't want to extend me the common courtesy of a phone call, Captain Reeves knew me. He and I go way back. The first person he should have been on the phone with was me once he realized Lia was my child.

"Hello, is Captain Reeves in?" I asked the receptionist.

"May I ask who you are?" she replied.

"You can tell him that Phil Robinson is here to see him."

***

Jack came out to greet me in no time. I guess he'd heard about Marco's death and knew that my being there had something to do with it. I wasn't in the mood for any politics today so I was going to make that perfectly clear.

"Hey, Phil, how have things been? How is Denise?" he asked while extending his hand.

I shook it. "She isn't doing to good and neither am I. I wish I could say I was here under better circumstances but the fact of the matter is I'm not. I need some answers that I'm sure you can provide."

He seemed puzzled. "Is there something wrong? Maybe we need to go into my office."

"Yeah, I think that would be a good idea."

I followed him back to his office. Once we were inside I didn't even waste any of his time with pleasantries.

"Jack, I want to know how the hell my daughter is interrogated by two of your detectives and not once do I get a phone call letting me know any of this. I'd expect that from some snot-nosed rookie but not you. We've got over twenty years of history together under our belt. The moment my daughter or her husband became a suspect, I should have been the first person you called. Now would you like to tell me what the hell was going on? How did Lia and Marco get dragged into this?"

"Phil, first of all, do not tell me how to run my got damn precinct. Now we might have known each other a long time but when you walk into someone's house, you better fucking respect it. This isn't any different. Respect my house or you'll quickly be shown the same front door you walked in through.

"Now, we were running an investigation and didn't need any leaks. If I would have called you, you wouldn't have come down here thinking like an investigator or a detective. You would have come down here thinking like a father who happened to be a detective."

"Okay, you might be right but I still deserved a call. What were they being investigated for?"

"Might I ask why this concerns you now? The last I heard her husband put a bullet in his head. Truth be told, the minute your daughter died so did any case against him."

"What do you mean?"

"Meaning, we had nothing really. We could place Mr. Reid at the scene hours earlier but according to records, his car was ticketed over on Market Street around the same time. That made things a little shaky. We also had a taped conversation with the victim and your daughter. It gave us a good motive but that was all.

"That son-in-law of yours, he wasn't ignorant to the situation at all. We threatened him with your daughter and he didn't even blink. The only shot we had of getting him was flipping your daughter against him."

"Well, if it makes you feel any better he confessed to the murder earlier today."

"Now I'm really lost. If that's the case, then why are you here seeking information?"

"Something just doesn't seem right, Jack. I mean, it seems too right if you know what I mean. We always raised our daughter to come to us about anything. Now if she was HIV positive, why would she think we would judge her? Who cares if she cheated? You ask me, I thought he was cheating on her long time ago but I left it alone. Now because she cheats she doesn't want her mother and me to know. Tell me what's wrong with that picture. Something just isn't right. I know one thing, I'm only getting one side of the story and right now that isn't enough for me. My daughter had no voice on that tape. Her voice came from him. I need to find out her voice from her."

"Well, Phil, I hate to tell you this but you'll never get her side the way you want to," Captain Reeves replied.

"I might not hear it from her mouth, but I'll get it. I'll find out the truth and that's all that matters."

I started to smirk.

"What is it?" Captain Reeves asked.

"You know that Marco is a cocky bastard. He played you and I think he is playing all of us too. At the end of his tape, he tells his brother Kenny to look within his heart for the answers to why he'd kill himself. Then he says in Spanish, *Nunca olvides, las cosas no son como suelen verse.*"

"So, what does that have to do with anything? He knows how to speak Spanish. Good for them."

"He said, never forget, everything isn't what it always seems. Now why would he tell his brother that in Spanish like he is trying to hide something? What isn't what it seems? Something isn't right, Jack, something isn't right. You should know by now there is your story, my story, and then the truth. I've heard his side of it. We're not getting Lia's so how about I just find out the truth!"

Author's Note

I hope you enjoyed this novel. I wanted to touch on two specific topics that we seem to ignore today. The first thing is depression. I have battled with depression, personally. I never truly understood how powerful it really is, until I went through it. The summer of 2005, I found myself dealing with a breakup between myself and the mother of my children. She was at the time the most important thing to me. Deep down, I knew I was depressed and thought it was just something I could deal with by myself. Then I took a good look at myself to see the full extent the depression had taken on me.

I wasn't eating. I wasn't sleeping. I wasn't doing anything but going to work every day and coming home. Days, weeks, months passed by and I didn't even know. I was just existing and not living. I didn't even notice how none of my clothes fit me any longer. They were all too big. I went from 187 to 131 pounds. That's a 50-pound loss and I had not one clue.

In my mind, I thought I was handling the breakup pretty good and was on the road to recovery. The fact of the matter was I wasn't. I needed help. This was something I couldn't do on my own. A lot of people don't really understand how serious depression really is.

If you find yourself down about anything, never feel as if you can't talk to someone. We all need that one person who we can talk to about whatever problems face us within our lives. Also, don't be too proud to seek the advice of a trained professional. Going to see a psychiatrist doesn't mean you are crazy.

Mine saved my life. I was very close to taking the easy road out. I tried to take my own life and found myself in the hospital wondering how I ever got to that point. How I ever ended up getting my stomach pumped trying to get out all the deadly toxins I'd put in my system.

I didn't care about all the people I'd hurt by taking my own life. I only saw the pain I was going through. I didn't think about how I have four children who rely and depend on me. How I have a nephew who loves me and a goddaughter who adores me. How I have a sister who is my twin and a mother who is my best friend. None of that crossed my mind until I allowed my psychiatrist to help me. A lot of employers now cover mental health, so please, please, please use the option if it's available to you.

The second thing I want to talk about is HIV and AIDS awareness. This book all started with a routine physical exam. I get tested for HIV and AIDS at least once a year. I thought this was a common practice for everyone. I didn't think I was in the minority and was doing something most don't. I didn't find that out until my last check-up and my doctor questioned my reasoning for routinely being checked.

I told him that I thought it was suggested by doctors to get tested at least once a year. He let me know that, though it is, most people don't do it. They only get tested if they are having high-risk sex. I'm no doctor but I thought as long as I was sexually active, condom or not, I take the risk of becoming infected. Therefore I felt it was my responsibility to get tested once a year.

Call me naïve, but I thought everyone felt the same way as I did. I decided to ask my family and friends. To my surprise the doctor was right. I asked my mother when the last time she was tested. She said she didn't need to get tested because she has her husband and that is a young person's disease. This is one of the smartest women I know saying one of the dumbest things I'd ever heard. I didn't know what to say. I figured why not prove her wrong.

I decided to do my research and according to the Centers for Disease Control (CDC) people in her age bracket are actually more likely to become infected than she thought. Also, the infection rate for black women her age was at a record high. My mother wasn't the only one who felt like this. I also asked a very close friend of mine and she told me she hadn't been tested since she was pregnant with her seven-year-old daughter. I couldn't believe what I was hearing.

These are two of the responsible people I know but they weren't responsible when it came to this issue. Then I came across a stat that was alarming and scary. One-third of all new HIV-positive cases don't know they are infected. I believe there were over two million reported new cases in 2002. If that number is accurate, that means you have 660,000 people who are HIV positive and have no clue. That is astonishing.

I think we are so relaxed as a society that since everyone knows about HIV and AIDS, we don't stress the importance of prevention all year-round. It used to be, that's all you would hear when this disease first hit the scene. Now I only hear about it during AIDS awareness week.

We can't get too relaxed, people. Get tested. I'm happy to say that I'm HIV negative but how would I have known my status if I never got tested. How could my partner feel safe? How can you if you don't know yours or your partner's? Let's do our part in the struggle against this disease, people. Don't be a follower. Break the cycle and start leading by example.

If you are having sex please protect yourself, start routinely getting tested for HIV and AIDS, and if you are HIV positive, don't think your life is over. The phrase, "Living with HIV," is a real way of life. Open your eyes and see!

About the Author

Harold L. Turley II was born and raised in Washington, D.C. An author and performance poet, he lives with his children in Fort Washington, Maryland. Turley first thrilled readers with the critically acclaimed novel *Love's Game*. His next novel is *Born Dying*. He is also a contributing author to *A Chocolate Seduction* and the upcoming *It's a Man's World*.

SNEAK PREVIEW! EXCERPT FROM

BORN DYING

BY **HAROLD L. TURLEY II**

COMING FROM STREBOR BOOKS DECEMBER 2007

THE BIRTH OF MONEY GREEN

CHAPTER 1

"Nate," a woman yelled from the other room in the house.

"Nate, get up! You are going to be late for school!"

I was dead tired from the night before and school was the last thought on my mind. I didn't feel like budging. Usually Momma would give me a courtesy wake-up call and then she would head straight for her bedroom where the comfort of her bed awaited her after a long night at work. Working ten-hour shifts for Telnet Wireless will do that to the average person. Momma didn't mind being the average person for a while but once she found out about my newfound habit to skip school, average was no longer a part of her title. She was determined to make sure I was where I needed to be whether it meant missing a couple of minutes or hours of sleep a day. She didn't care. School was priority number one in her book.

"Nathaniel Dante Rodgers, if you do not get your skinny ass out of that bed you will be wearing those sheets to your funeral next week," she said as she shook my bed to make sure I'd get up.

"Damn Ma, I'm up!"

"Excuse you? Who the hell do you think you are talking to? If you want to cuss in this house, then you need to go through nine months of pregnancy, forty-six hours of labor, and pay the household bills. When you do all that, then you can cuss in this house. Other than that you will respect me and my house or I will knock your ass on the floor. Are we clear?"

The smirk that painted my face showed that I understood her completely but also took part of what was said as a joke. My mother never had a problem playing tough, but when it came time to lay down the law physically she was nothing but a pussy cat.

"Boy, if you don't wipe that damn smirk off your face."

I cut her off, "I know, I know. You are going to knock me into the middle of next week."

I couldn't help but laugh after repeating a saying my mother said over and over again.

"I'm sorry, Ma, it will never happen again. I was half asleep."

"What have I told you about saying you are 'sorry'? I didn't have a 'sorry' child."

"Excuse me, I meant, I apologize. Now if you don't mind, Mother, can you excuse me so I can get dressed?"

"Boy, I've seen what you have. I'm the one who diapered that little thing of yours."

"Ma, there is nothing little about my thing."

Now she had found something to be amused about. She broke out into laughter.

"Child, please, at fourteen years old, everything is little on your butt except your heart. That is the only thing big any fourteen-year-old can have. Now let's get ready for school so you can continue to expand your mind."

I started to get out of the bed.

"I'll let your little comment slide since you are my mother and I love you, but don't let it happen again. I know a couple of girls who would disagree with you though."

That caught my mother off guard and she now was intrigued.

"Oh really, is that right? Keep digging and your hole will continue to get deeper and deeper. After a while, it will be too deep for you to get out of it."

"It was a joke, Ma. I didn't mean anything behind it. I was just pushing your buttons like always. There is nothing to be worried about."

She wasn't buying it. "I bet. I know one thing, if you are dumb enough to be poking that thing around, you better be smart enough to know you need to be wearing a condom as well."

"Ma, come on! It's really not that serious. It was a joke."

"Don't 'come on Ma' me and don't brush off what I'm saying either. I'm serious, Nathaniel. It's too much shit traveling around out in these streets and I don't need you bringing any of it into this house.

"Things aren't like they were when I was growing up. Then all you had to worry about was possibly getting pregnant. But now, now you have to worry about saving your life. One night unprotected these days can cost you just that."

I knew the only way this conversation would ever end would be if I ignored her. If I assured her I was using protection, she'd want to know more about my sex life such as when, where, and the most important, who. If I said I wasn't using protection she'd question as to why not, run down all the possible diseases I could contract, then would start up with the when, where, and who. Telling her I wasn't active at all wasn't working so I decided it was time to get ready for school. I just looked at her with my hazel eyes and my mouth closed.

"Do you hear me talking to you?" she questioned.

I nodded my head yes so I wasn't being totally disrespectful but didn't answer the question she wanted answered either.

She became frustrated. "It's too early in the morning to be going through this and I'm too tired. Get your butt up and get ready for school."

I knew that wouldn't be the last of that conversation but at least it was for today. My mother finally left my room. I made a mental note to get an alarm clock later on that day to make sure she didn't have to wake me up anymore to avoid these types of talks.

It's cool being able to talk to your mother but you don't want to talk to her about every damn thing. I headed for my closet to pull out an outfit to wear to school. I grabbed a pair of blue jeans and a white T-shirt.

By the time I got out of the shower and dressed, my mother was fast asleep. I walked into her room and put the covers over top of her, then gave her a kiss on the forehead. I made sure to put $200 in her purse and hoped she used it for something regarding the house.

I always made it a habit to slip money into my mother's purse. I just put it in the middle of whatever cash she had in her wallet so it didn't stand out. Sometimes, I'd mix it in with other bills depending on the amount. It was a lot easier to hide $50 in the middle than $200. I spread the two fifties and one one-hundred dollar bill around so it wasn't obvious. It obviously was working because up-to-date, she hadn't asked me anything about it. Had she been suspicious the questions she really didn't want answers to would have come by now.

I walked into Oxon Hill High School in Oxon Hill, Maryland and headed straight for my locker. My morning schedule was crazy. I had English, Geometry, and Spanish. And all of them were before I even had lunch. I don't know who chose my schedule but surely it wasn't me. P.E. would have been slid somewhere in between that load if I had done my schedule.

To my surprise, O'Neal was standing at my locker waiting on me. O'Neal and I went back since pee wee football. He was my best friend and business partner. He was never real big on school so whenever I saw him there, it was a shock to me. He was only a year older than me but we both were in the same grade.

"Are you ready to break out?" he asked.

"We don't have a job?"

"What's your point, Nate?"

"My point is I can't fuck with it today. It's one thing to roll and make some extra change. But it's a whole different ball game to fuck up in school, cause my mother to get suspicious to what I'm doing, and eventually mess with my paper trail all because I wanted to break camp just for the hell of it."

"Keep your pager on then because you know how Chico is. When work needs to be put in, he doesn't factor your English test into consideration." O'Neal extended his hand to dap me up. "I might stick around for a few to try to catch up with the shortie we bumped in to last night. If not, I'll just catch up with you around the way later."

"That sounds like a plan."

I grabbed my books out of my locker and headed to class. School really was just something for me to do to pass the time by. I wasn't real big on it only because wasn't shit going to be taught to me that I was going to use in my line of work.

I'd already been taught how to add, subtract, multiply, and divide so I had the basics I needed. Adding or multiplying my paper stack was all that mattered. If subtractions had to be factored in, then I was doing something wrong. The division part, well there was both O'Neal and I so dividing by two was fine by me.

At this point, school wasn't for me anymore. It was now mostly to please my mother. I'd do anything to make that woman happy. She had been through enough with losing my father in the '80s to drugs and I didn't need to add to her problems. I did what I had to do to make sure I got acceptable grades. I didn't want to stand out so if I got a couple of A's or B's I made sure to have a few D's on there as well, so there was always something to improve upon in her eyes.

I walked into the cafeteria after my brutal morning schedule ready to relax. To my surprise, O'Neal was still at school. I knew he'd never leave and come back all in one day. If he was out, I wouldn't see him anymore until we met up after school around the way. There was only one thing that could have kept him at school and she was standing right next to him as he was throwing on his charm.

I walked over to the back of the cafeteria where they were standing. He was in prime form. Pussy was always on his mind. That, if not his temper, would be his biggest downfall.

"What's good? I thought you were breaking camp earlier. Why the change of heart?" I asked O'Neal even though I already knew the answer. He gave me a look to say 'stop frontin' like you don't know.'

"I had some things I needed to take care of first. Have you met Nikki?"

"Naw, not formally but I've seen her around a couple of times before. You live in Forest Heights, right?"

"Damn, are you stalking me or something?" she said defensively.

I was insulted by her remark. She was cute but not my taste at all.

"Bitch, please! Don't flatter yourself because it's not that serious!" I snapped back.

O'Neal put his hand over his head knowing the conversation from that point on was going nowhere but downhill.

"Who the fuck is you calling a bitch?"

"Calm down, boo! He didn't mean it like that," O'Neal said, trying to defuse the situation.

"Y'all niggas must have me twisted if you think I'm just going to sit here and let you talk to me any ole way. You best believe someone will be addressing this shit later on," she said, then stormed off before either of us could reply.

We both knew what she meant but it wasn't fazing either of us. The damage had been done and when it came time to bump heads with them Forest Heights niggas, we'd be more than ready.

"Damn, nigga, when are you going to learn to control your mouth? You can't just say whatever comes to mind, especially when it's going to interfere with my action."

I couldn't help but laugh at that. O'Neal never let anything come between him and some action unless it was money.

"My bad I didn't mean to throw a monkey wrench in your plans, seriously. But Slim came out the mouth wrong with that dumb shit and she needed to be put back in her place quick. Don't even fake like you don't know! What do I look like stalking some body let alone her ass?"

O'Neal found that very funny. "I was stalking her ass though. Why didn't you tell me last night you knew where Slim stayed? I could have used that information."

"For what? I knew you'd find a way to catch up with her on your own and not look like you were pressed. How does that look? You are never around Forest Heights, don't live around there, but just happened to be around there to get at Slim. Come on, that isn't original at all. Naw, you needed to catch up with her at school or wherever and then play your hand."

"Yeah, you are right. Damn, it's about that time though. We need to get up out of here."

"For what? I know you aren't tripping off that bullshit-ass threat."

"Come on now, you should know me better than that. When have I ever run from a fight? We have to be out because we have a meeting with Chico. He hit me up this morning."

I was dumbfounded because I didn't get a page from him but knew not to ask any questions. Chico was the one putting money in our pockets so if he called a meeting, I was definitely going to be there.

"Did he say what it was about?"

"No and I really didn't want to know either. The only thing I needed to know was bread and he always provides that so I'm good."

O'Neal turned toward the double doors leading outside and headed through them. I wasn't too far behind him. The way our school was built, the cafeteria was at the front of the school and led straight to the parking lot and where the school buses dropped off and picked up students.

Usually there were security guards out there but they were just there as props. They broke up the occasional fight here and there but that was about it. They didn't give a damn who left school early or why. Half the time, they were trying to get the girls to leave early with them for some lunchtime fun.

Chico's black Lincoln Town car pulled up at the bottom of the steps in the parking lot. We headed straight for it.

"What's going on, Chico?" O'Neal said the minute he got in the car.

"Hurry up and close the door. We have business to attend to."

I cut straight through the chase.

"How do we factor into your business plans today?"

Chico found my bluntness amusing.

"Always the straight shooter, huh, Nate? I like that."

Chico was a small-time dealer under the Cardoza crime family. Anyone who knew anything knew Mario was the man to know in the metropolitan area. He held all the power in D.C. and Chico was my steppingstone up the ladder to him. O'Neal was only along for the small-time paper we were making now. To a couple of fourteen- and sixteen-year-olds, $600 a week was a lot of money, especially to only be runners.

I had bigger plans though. I just needed to find a way to make them happen. I was a true believer that time and patience would open all the doors we needed to succeed. You just had to wait until your opportunity presented itself to you, then seize your moment and not waste it. That was something I was determined to do.

"Chico, my style will never change. I'm always going to be about that paper."

"Well, little homie, if you handle this job right, you will do just that. I've got something new for the both of you. Are you game?"

"Is money green?"

"My man! That is exactly what I wanted to hear. Okay, here is the deal. Nate, there is a bag underneath my seat so before you get out of the car make sure you slide over and get it. Don't be all obvious and shit either. Just make your way over to my side a little before I get to Eastover and then just get out on my side of the car. O'Neal, there is a pistol under your seat. Make sure you reach under and get that as well.

"I'm sure I don't have to school you on how to keep a piece on you. You make sure nothing happens to that damn bag. Now, I'm going to drop both of you off at Eastover, then this is what I want you to do. You need to take the bag to Wayne Place in Southeast. It's not that far of a walk from Eastover but it's also going to be good exercise as well.

"When you get on Wayne, ask for Tony. I'm sure someone out there will point you in the right direction. Once you catch up with Tony, let him know you have his weekly delivery. He'll have another bag to give you. I'll meet the both of you back where I drop you off at in an hour and a half. If you are late, that is your ass. If anything is missing from either bag that is your ass.

"O'Neal, any sign of ANY problems, don't hesitate to use that pistol or that will be your ass. Notice I said use and not pull out, this is not show and tell. If it comes out, there better be some noise following behind it too.

"I can't stress this enough, I don't care which one comes back but either my product or my cash needs to be back here with you. If you have to bring the product back, so be it. We can always do the deal at a later time if need be. Are we clear?"

By the tone of Chico's voice, this wasn't the normal run. We'd moved up to something more serious than the one or two pounds of marijuana he'd have us drop off at the normal hot spots. Now he had us crossing the D.C. line which wasn't even his territory. We were restricted to Maryland only. One thing bothered me about the whole situation though and it was something that needed to be addressed.

"What's Tony's price? I don't like not knowing that, especially when it's my ass on the line. You telling us to make sure nothing is missing from either bag but if this nigga shorts us, we won't know because we don't even know how much to expect. I'm not feeling that. I want to make sure every dollar is in there before I head out of that spot."

Chico could see the problem facing us. Though he doubted Tony would ever try to go up against the family, anything was possible. Especially if all he had to say was he gave us the right payment and our hands got itchy. There would be no way to disprove that. It would be his word against ours and with him being the client he'd have more leverage, especially if we wasn't known to get over.

"Good point, lil' homie, very good point. It is smarter if you count the money before you roll to make sure we aren't being stiffed. Respect is everything so make sure he understands it's for precaution reasons only and not out of disrespect. You wanting to count the money is only business.

"There should be 14K in the bag. Anything under that, you walk your ass up out of there with our product in hand. Is that clear?"

"Crystal!"

hico dropped us off in front of the Midas Brake Shop next to the Popeye's in Eastover Shopping Mall in Oxon Hill, Maryland. It was right next to the Southeast D.C. line. Before I got out of the car, I made sure to look and see what time the clock in Chico's car read.

By it, it was 1:22 p.m. I set my watch to 1:24 p.m. to give me a two-minute cushion. I wasn't going to risk getting my ass whipped, shot, or worse all because I was five minutes late. It wasn't going down like that. No, I was going to make sure we were back by 2:45 p.m.

I knew exactly how to get to Wayne Place so that was the easy part, and I had an idea of where to find Tony. The walk to our destination was a quiet one. We both were a little nervous because neither of us knew what to expect. We didn't know these niggas or what they were capable of. You hear about deals going bad all the time and the one's usually doing the drop-off are the ones you see on the news being zipped up in body bags.

I kept replaying every possible scenario over in my head to avoid that. My nerves reached full tilt when we finally made it to Wanye Place. I looked at my watch to check the time and it was 1:47 p.m. That was good to know. It only took us twenty-three minutes to get here so with the same amount of time going back we needed to be leaving by at least 2:22 p.m. We had good time to spare. I stopped walking.

"What's wrong?" O'Neal questioned.

"Nothing, look, when we get there let me do all the talking. When I go to count the money, I'm going to give you this bag to hold until everything is gravy. Make sure you keep your eyes and ears open at all times. You are the only nigga I trust with my life in this world so you better make damn sure I leave this place with it."

"Champ, from the cradle to the grave. You know I have your back."

"Okay, we have about fifteen minutes to be in and out. Hopefully they don't try to hit us with no bullshit because of our ages."

"Fuck them!"

We walked up the block to a building that read 3915. There were four men on the front stoop playing craps. That's when it kicked in; the easy time I was hoping for wasn't going to happen.

"I'm looking for Tony."

A short, but stocky, light-skinned brother broke away from the game. He looked me over quickly and assumed I was a fein or something.

"You'll find what you need across the street."

"If Tony isn't over there then I won't find shit. Now if you're not Tony, can you do both of us a favor and point me in the right direction so I can conclude my business?"

He cracked a brief smile on his face.

"Listen to this little mutha fucka. Who do you think you are talking to? Do you even know where your ass is at?"

O'Neal started to become a little anxious and was easing his hand toward his pistol. I looked at him to let him know it was cool.

"Man, fuck all that, I have business with the man. How about this, when you see him you let him know his weekly delivery came by but you told the little mutha fucka to head across the street instead." I turned to O'Neal and said, "Come on, we are out!"

"Hold up!" I heard someone say from behind us. I turned around to face him.

A tall brown, skinny brother with cornrows was now standing up. From the looks of the cash in his hand, he was cleaning house in the crap game.

"The kid they call Chico sent you?" he asked.

"I don't know who that is, just like I don't know who you are either. Y'all fellas have a good day."

I turned to leave again.

"Okay, my man, you made your point. I'm Tony."

"Then you are the man I came to see. Now can we get to business, please? I have other shit to do with my time."

The short stocky guy cut me off.

"What the fuck does your little ass have to do?"

I ignored him and looked Tony dead in his eyes.

"After you," I suggested,

"No problem, your boy can wait down here with the fellas."

"No disrespect but again, I don't know y'all. Where I go, he goes."

I looked at my watch to check the time. It was already 2:01 p.m. Time was flying by. By me looking at my watch though, it gave the illusion that my time was precious and they were running out of it if they wanted to make this deal happen. Though that wasn't what I was trying to portray, it was the tactic that did just the trick.

"Okay, come on," he agreed.

We followed Tony into the building and up the stairs. O'Neal was looking over his shoulder the whole time. I don't think he liked the fact that the same guy with all the damn mouth and attitude downstairs was following behind him up the steps. This whole situation was nerve-wracking but a needed experience. Tony stopped at Apartment B2 and knocked twice.

A dark-skinned guy opened the door and let us in. At a quick glimpse, I didn't think this was where they stored the product. I was starting to get very nervous because everything was saying "set up."

The dark-skinned guy who opened the door headed straight for the couch to take a seat and finish watching *Jerry Springer* on TV. Tony went into the back room. Once he came out, he had a small black bag in his hand. I didn't know much about $14,000 up close and personal but that bag seemed a little too small to be carrying it.

"Do you mind if I count it first?"

"This little nigga has balls," the stocky guy said.

I could see I needed to ease the tension. We were halfway home and I didn't need the deal going sour because Tony felt like he was being bullied by a kid in front of his boys.

"Again, I don't mean any disrespect but the people I work for will have my ass if it's not 14K in that bag."

"Moe, chill the fuck out! Little man, it's no problem. I'd want to count it too if I were in your shoes. The first rule of business always will be you can't trust anyone in this game, everyone has their own agenda."

Tony handed me the bag after I handed the product to O'Neal to hold so I could count the money. I was sure all three of them had pistols on them or in the apartment somewhere so they had to feel comfortable we wouldn't try to run out with the money and the product in hand. I didn't waste any time. I quickly counted the one-hundred and forty hundred-dollar bills. I looked at O'Neal.

"We good."

He handed the product to Tony. He opened the bag and pulled out what seemed to be a key of cocaine. Tony gave the bag to the dark-skinned guy so he could verify the product was good. Once he gave Tony the nod everything was cool, O'Neal and I were out the door.

$$$

We stuck to the main roads the entire way back to Eastover which took us a little longer. In my opinion you could never be too cautious and my antennas were up. I didn't trust Moe. My gut kept telling me he would try to find a way to get over on us and hit our heads for the 14K we just got up off them.

He seemed like the scheming type. I figured he was either following us back or put the word out that we were out on the street with that type of cash. I didn't take Tony for the type. He seemed more like a man who didn't want to mess up a good thing but he could always deny knowing anything about us being robbed if it came down to it, pocket the cash, and the key he was sold. Chico had made it clear what the repercussions were if we didn't come back with either the product or the cash.

Once we made it back to Eastover, we still had a good ten minutes to spare before Chico came to pick up the cash so we sat inside the Popeye's chicken spot and waited. It was next to the Midas Brake Shop and the parking lot was in plain view so we wouldn't miss Chico.

Like clockwork, Chico pulled up in the parking lot at 2:45 p.m. The minute we spotted the Lincoln, I headed out to meet him while O'Neal waited inside. By the time I reached the car, the trunk was already popped. I opened it, placed the bag inside the trunk, and then closed it. Chico backed out of the parking spot he was occupying and then drove off. The transaction was finally completed.

GREG STIER

FACE YOUR FEARS AND FUEL YOUR PASSION

EVANGE PHOBIA

DEVOTIONAL

Evangephobia: Facing Your Fears and Fueling Your Passion

group.com
simplyyouthministry.com

Credits
Author: Greg Stier
Executive Developer: Nadim Najm
Chief Creative Officer: Joani Schultz
Editors: Jane Dratz and Rob Cunningham
Art Director: Veronica Lucas
Production Manager: DeAnne Lear

ISBN 978-0-7644-6670-0

10 9 8 7 6 5 4 3 2 1   20 19 18 17 16 15 14 13 12 11

Printed in the United States of America.